MONTANA BRIDES

Welcome to Montana—a place of passion and adventure, where there is a charming little town with some big secrets…

Emma Stover: Since her arrival, Emma has met her evil birth mother Lexine…and the man of her dreams. But stolen nights of passion and Emma's family history didn't add up to happily ever after. Particularly when she was arrested for the murder of Christina Montgomery…

Brandon Harper: Kincaid heir Brandon doesn't believe in marriage and family ties, but he does trust that his passion for Emma is more real than anything else in his increasingly surreal world. So when the handcuffs were clasped, Brandon did the inconceivable: he united the Kincaid family to come to Emma's defence.

Audra Westwood: When twin Emma is arrested, Audra hopes her plot to stay out of her own prison cell has succeeded…

Max Montgomery: Max puts up a small fortune to capture the killer who'd claimed his baby sister's life…

The
Birth
Mother

PAMELA TOTH

V ™ SILHOUETTE®

Silhouette and Colophon are registered trademarks of Harlequin Books S.A., used under licence.

First published in Great Britain 2001.
Silhouette Books, Eton House, 18-24 Paradise Road,
Richmond, Surrey TW9 1SR

© Harlequin Books S.A. 2000

Special thanks and acknowledgement are given to Pamela Toth for her contribution to the Montana Brides series.

ISBN 0 373 65053 1

19-0102

Printed and bound in Spain
by Litografia Rosés S.A., Barcelona

PAMELA TOTH

USA Today best-selling author Pamela Toth was born in Wisconsin, but grew up in Seattle, where she attended the University of Washington and specialised in art. She has two daughters, Erika and Melody, and two Siamese cats.

Recently she took a lead from one of her own romances and married her school sweetheart, Frank. They live in a town house—with a fabulous view of Mount Rainier—within walking distance of a bookshop and an ice cream shop, two of life's necessities. When she's not writing, Pamela enjoys travelling with her husband, reading, playing computer games, doing counted cross-stitch and researching new story ideas. She's been an active member of Romance Writers of America since 1982.

Her books have won several awards and they claim regular spots on best-selling romance lists. She loves hearing from readers and can be reached at PO Box 436, Woodinville, WA 98072, USA.

To the men of the West and the women
who love them!

MONTANA BRIDES

Twelve rich tales of passion and adventure,
of secrets about to be told...

MONTANA BRIDES
THE KINCAIDS

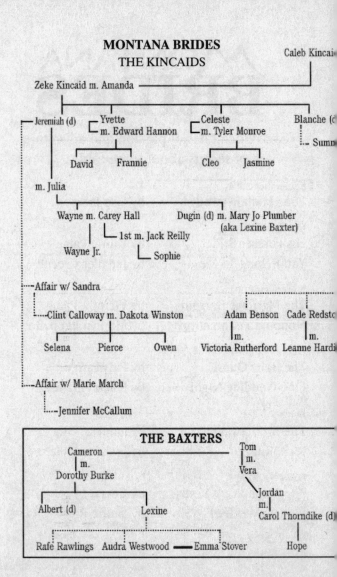

Caleb Kincai(

Zeke Kincaid m. Amanda

Jeremiah (d)

Yvette
m. Edward Hannon

Celeste
m. Tyler Monroe

Blanche (d

Summ

David   Frannie

Cleo   Jasmine

m. Julia

Wayne m. Carey Hall   Dugin (d) m. Mary Jo Plumber
(aka Lexine Baxter)

1st m. Jack Reilly

Wayne Jr.

Sophie

Affair w/ Sandra

Clint Calloway m. Dakota Winston   Adam Benson Cade Redsto

m.   m.

Selena   Pierce   Owen   Victoria Rutherford Leanne Hardi

Affair w/ Marie March

Jennifer McCallum

THE BAXTERS

Cameron   Tom
m.   m.
Dorothy Burke   Vera

Jordan
m.

Albert (d)   Lexine   Carol Thorndike (d)

Hope

Rafe Rawlings Audra Westwood — Emma Stover

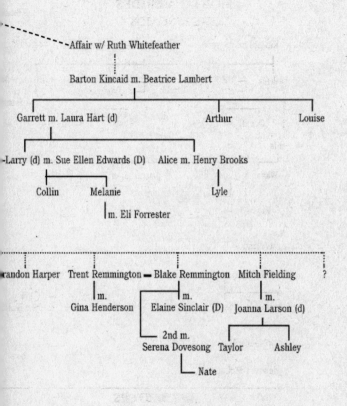

‑‑‑Affair w/ Ruth Whitefeather

Barton Kincaid m. Beatrice Lambert

Garrett m. Laura Hart (d)   Arthur   Louise

‑Larry (d) m. Sue Ellen Edwards (D) Alice m. Henry Brooks

Collin Melanie   Lyle

m. Eli Forrester

randon Harper Trent Remmington — Blake Remmington Mitch Fielding ?

m.   m.   m.
Gina Henderson Elaine Sinclair (D) Joanna Larson (d)

2nd m.
Serena Dovesong Taylor Ashley

Nate

Symbols
..... Child of an Affair
— Twins
d Deceased
D Divorced

Prologue

"I hope your wife feels better." Emma Stover watched the cook tuck the bank deposit bag into the floor safe and then she followed him to the front door of the Hip Hop Café.

"Thanks for closing up," he replied. "Everything's clean, so all you have left to do is the table setups. Are you working the breakfast shift tomorrow?"

"No, lunch and dinner." Emma had been a waitress at the café for several months now. Usually she worked earlier in the day, but one of the other waitresses was out sick.

The cook hesitated in the doorway. "Lock the door after me. And thanks again."

After he'd left, Emma hurriedly finished her chores. She didn't like being the last one here. Even though it wasn't even 10:00 p.m. on a hot August night, this part of Whitehorn was already a ghost town.

She was perfectly safe, she told herself a few minutes later as she pushed her glasses back up the bridge of her nose, grabbed her purse and turned off the lights. She just wished she'd thought to park at the side of the building instead of out back in the alley. At least she didn't have to worry about her car starting. Tired of begging rides from Janie Austin, the manager, whenever it let her down, she'd had a new battery installed the week before. Though she rented a garage apartment from Janie and her husband, the two women didn't always work the same shift.

Taking a deep breath, Emma went outside and locked the front door. As she turned to the sidewalk, the figure of a man appeared suddenly, blocking her path. The streetlight was behind him, shadowing his face as he confronted her.

Frightened, Emma clutched the keys like a weapon and opened her mouth to scream.

"I've been waiting for you," the man said, turning slightly so the light caught the side of his face.

"Brandon!" she yelped in relief, her knees nearly buckling as she clapped her free hand over her thundering heart. "You scared the heck out of me!"

Brandon Harper caught her arms as she swayed. "Damn, I'm sorry. I only meant to surprise you. Are you okay?"

"Yes, of course." Embarrassed, Emma managed a weak laugh as he let her go. Her glasses had slid down her nose again, so she pushed them back up as she stared.

Even in the poor light, black-haired Brandon's angular face was devilishly attractive. He towered over Emma, making her feel ridiculously petite instead of just boringly average in height. The other waitresses teased her when he came in to eat, insisting he sat at her station deliberately, but she hadn't seen him in weeks. For some reason he'd been on her mind today as she pictured the quiet intensity of his gaze and the sensual curve of his mouth. She'd wondered whether she would ever see him again and now here he was as though she'd conjured him up herself.

She was so relieved that she wanted to touch him to make sure he was real. "I'm sorry," she said instead, tucking the keys into the pocket of her uniform shorts. "I don't usually close up by myself, so I guess I was a little nervous. I didn't mean to overreact."

"Don't apologize," Brandon replied, his deep voice as smooth as the surface of a lake on a still evening. "I was the one who should have had more sense than to jump out at you the way I did."

"Why are you here?" Emma blurted.

His teeth flashed white in the gloom. "To see you, of course."

For a moment she felt like Red Riding Hood in the presence of the wolf. The last time he'd come into the café he asked her to join him on her break. She'd enjoyed talking to him, but she'd also understood that he was only passing the time with her. Even dressed casually as he was now in a black shirt and jeans, Brandon exuded self-assurance like an expensive cologne. Men like him didn't fall for plain-Jane waitresses. It was just as well. He might make Emma's heart race, but a relationship—even a casual one— was a complication her life had no room for right now.

"How have you been?" she asked, doing her best to ignore the way the streetlight threw his cheekbones into harsh relief and brightened the blue of his eyes.

"Busy," he replied. "I've been out of town on business since the last time I saw you."

That explained why he hadn't been around. He'd never said much, but Emma knew he had business interests in Nevada and a family here in Whitehorn. In fact, it was only a few months ago that Brandon was told he was an illegitimate grandson of Garrett Kincaid—the patriarch of Whitehorn's most well-known family.

"Welcome back." She twisted her hands together, wishing she could think of a witty comment. He must know women who were a lot more clever than Emma. She was out of her depth. Even so, vanity made her regret her untidy ponytail and work uniform of black shorts and blue T-shirt with Breakfast Served All Day printed across the front. Just once she'd like him to see her in flattering clothes and non-sensible shoes.

"It's nice to be back." Each word he spoke was a velvet caress.

Emma swallowed a sigh. If she wasn't careful, she'd make a fool of herself. "I shouldn't keep you." She wished she had the nerve to ask how long he'd be in town this time.

"Would you like to go somewhere for a drink?" he asked, shocking her.

Was it possible he'd been serious about coming to see her? Emma was almost unbearably tempted to accept his offer, but then reality hit like a dash of cold water. He was just being polite.

"I'd better not. The café was busy tonight and I'm pretty tired. I wouldn't be very good company."

He shoved his hands into his pockets, wide shoulders slightly hunched, and glanced down at his feet. He was probably trying to hide his relief that she hadn't embarrassed them both by accepting. "Sure, I understand." He raised his head and looked around. "Where did you park? The least I can do is escort you to your car."

Emma noticed his sleek dark sedan sitting alone in the customer lot like a panther waiting to spring. "I'm parked around back." Instead of pining like a teen with an unrequited crush, she should be grateful he was considerate enough to walk her down the deserted alley.

In silence Emma led the way around the building to where her old green Chevy waited in the shadows. He walked alongside her, grasping her elbow briefly when she stumbled on the loose gravel. His fingers were warm against her bare skin, but he let her go almost immediately after she mumbled her thanks.

He waited patiently while she unlocked her door and then he held it open for her as she climbed behind the wheel. Flustered by his gallant gesture, she rolled down her window to thank him.

"No problem," he replied, peering at her in the gloom. "Have a good night." He stepped back expectantly, obviously waiting for her to pull away.

Her hands were shaking, so it took two tries to find the ignition with her key. When she turned it, nothing happened. Frowning, she jiggled the gearshift lever and tried again. This wasn't supposed to happen.

"Trouble?" Brandon asked.

Disgusted, Emma slapped the steering wheel and leaned back in the seat. "It won't start," she admitted, fighting sudden tears. But the mechanic had been so sure a new battery was all she needed.

"Let me try." He opened her door. "Slide over."

If it had been any other man but Brandon, Emma might have resented the implication that being male made him automatically more skilled at starting a car. Instead she was just grateful that she wasn't stuck here by herself. Quickly she moved over so he could get in beside her. He seemed to fill the interior of the car with his presence, so Emma pressed closer to the passenger door.

The engine was no more responsive to Brandon's touch than it had been to hers. "Maybe it's the battery," he suggested after he'd tried the key a second time with equally unspectacular results.

"No, it can't be. I just bought a new one."

Brandon stared through the windshield for a moment while Emma chewed her lip. No doubt he was wishing he'd steered a wide berth around the café tonight.

"I suppose even new batteries can go bad. I'm no mechanic, but I guess I can take a look. Do you have a flashlight?"

She dug around in the glove box and handed him one, feeling guilty for taking up even more of his time. "I appreciate this," she said in a small voice.

"No problem." Fumbling for the latch, he raised the hood and shone the light over the engine as she moved back behind the wheel. Perhaps some wire had come loose.

"Find anything?" she called through the open window. Please, she muttered anxiously, mindful of the pathetic state of her finances, let it be something cheap.

"You say you just bought a new battery?" he asked, an odd note in his voice.

"That's right." Maybe they'd hooked it up wrong.

"It's not here."

"What?" Emma frowned as his words sank in, and then she scooted out of the car to peer under the hood herself. There was an empty space next to the engine. "It's gone," she said foolishly.

"At least we know why the car wouldn't start." As she stood back, he shut the hood, gave it an experimental tug and switched off the flashlight. "Get your purse and lock the doors. I'll take you home."

"Oh, no, that's not necessary," she babbled. "I can call someone else." Would Janie still be up? It couldn't be much after ten o'clock. "I don't want to take you out of your way."

"Don't be silly. I'm not going to leave you here." Brandon sounded impatient, making her feel even worse. "Where do you live?"

It would probably be quicker to agree than to continue arguing. "My apartment's a ten-minute drive."

Except for brief directions, Emma couldn't think of anything to say on the way and Brandon barely spoke. As she sank into the luxurious leather of his Lexus and listened to something low, slow and seductive

ooze from his stereo, she wished the short trip would
never end.

Too soon he turned onto her street. "It's the next
driveway," she said. "My apartment is over the garage behind the house." The street was empty, the
neighborhood quiet except for the distant growl of a
motorcycle.

Brandon parked on the other side of the garage,
away from the house. She'd expected him to wait
with the engine running while she went up the stairs
to her door. Instead he shut it off and got out of the
car.

"Would you like to come in?" she asked after he
had circled the car to let her out. Good thing she'd
washed the dishes that morning and taken down the
underwear hanging in the bathroom. "The least I can
do is to give you a cup of coffee or a glass of iced
tea for all your trouble."

"It was no trouble," he replied, "but something
cold to drink does sound good."

Before Emma knew how it happened, they were
seated on the Hide-A-Bed sofa in her tiny apartment
and she was explaining why she'd come to Whitehorn. Once she relaxed, talking to Brandon was easy.
Perhaps it was because he was such a good listener,
his gaze steady on her face as though he found her
fascinating.

She didn't usually tell people the truth about herself—that she'd been raised in foster homes—but he
wormed it out of her with his questions. Then he
dumbfounded her by admitting that he, too, had

grown up as a ward of the court. He didn't elaborate, but Emma figured he'd understand her real reason for coming to Whitehorn.

"Three months ago I came here to find my birth mother," she blurted. Belatedly she realized she'd been talking his ear off while his glass sat empty. Her cheeks flamed with embarrassment as she leaped to her feet. "I didn't mean to go on like that. Let me refill this."

Before she could escape into her minuscule kitchen with his glass, Brandon stood and blocked her way. "You didn't tell me whether you found her," he said softly, resting his hands on Emma's shoulders to stop her flight.

She stared at the solid wall of his chest and breathed in his scent. "Who?" she asked blankly.

He chuckled. "Your birth mother."

Lifting her gaze to his face, Emma considered what she'd so recently learned about the woman who'd given her life. Just because Emma and Brandon shared a history didn't mean she was prepared to tell him about Lexine Baxter. "I'm getting closer," she hedged.

His grin widened and he squeezed her shoulders. "Good girl. That must make you happy."

She couldn't admit to her mixed emotions without explaining the situation. "It's hard to believe you were a foster child," she said, desperate to change the subject.

He cocked his head. "Why is that?"

His question surprised her. The answer seemed so

obvious. "Because you're so—" Flustered, she tried
again. "You don't seem—" Why hadn't she kept her
mouth shut?

"Yes?"

Emma wriggled from his grasp and ducked around
him. "I'll get that iced tea."

Brandon caught up with her in the kitchen before
she could open the door of the old-fashioned refrigerator. The room was barely big enough for the two
of them. He took the empty glass from her hand and
set it down. Stepping back, Emma bumped the
counter behind her.

Brandon was watching her with a quizzical smile.
"I'm still waiting."

She stared up at him. His haircut alone probably
cost more than she cleared in tips in a week. "I can't
explain."

He looked disappointed. "I'm just a man, Emma.
I laugh, I hurt. I get lonely like everyone else."

She couldn't imagine someone like Brandon Harper being alone unless he wanted it that way. He'd
mentioned his family. From what she'd heard about
Garrett Kincaid, he was a welcoming sort. Was it possible Brandon struggled with the same doubts and in-
securities as she did? Not very likely. Before she
could think of a way to ask, he leaned closer and his
gaze drifted to her mouth.

The air in the kitchen crackled with sudden tension.
Emma's eyes widened at the intent in his. "Are you
going to kiss me?" she blurted.

"If it's all right with you," he responded gravely.

She swallowed as he cupped her chin with his fingers. Her pulse fluttered erratically. She must have fallen asleep in her car and now she was dreaming.

"Emma? May I?"

"Yes, please," she whispered, realizing that, asleep or awake, she craved Brandon Harper's kiss as much as just about anything else she had ever wanted in her life.

One

Brandon Harper pulled his black Lexus into an empty space in the Hip Hop Café parking lot and cut the engine. While he waited for an old woman to climb stiffly from the car on his left, he tucked his cell phone into his jacket pocket and glanced with a bemused expression at the bunch of flowers lying on the seat next to him.

On this beautiful April day he'd driven up to Whitehorn from Reno instead of flying just to give himself some time to think, and he'd brought the yellow roses as a peace offering for the waitress he'd left so abruptly the last time he'd seen her. He knew he should have called Emma before now, but he'd been busy. No sooner had he put out one fire at work than another flared up.

While he'd debated what he wanted to say to her, a month had slipped by, and then another. Postponing the call had gotten easier. By the time he'd come to Whitehorn for the holidays, seeing her would have been awkward, involving explanations he hadn't been prepared to give.

He'd assumed she would fade from his mind like an outdated stock market prediction. She certainly wasn't his usual type, but he found himself thinking about her at the oddest times—wondering how she was, what she was doing. Whom she was spending her time with.

Unfinished business always made Brandon a little nervous, so he'd finally decided to find out whether his mind had been playing tricks on him or if Emma was truly as sweet as he remembered. As tempting.

As unforgettable.

She had good reason to be upset with him, he conceded. The last time he'd been with her, he was summoned back to Reno for an early morning meeting with a nervous investor over a deal that threatened to turn as sour as outdated milk. Thinking back, Brandon should have chartered a plane instead of driving, but he hadn't been thinking too clearly at the time.

Emma had been a virgin. That hot late August night in her apartment he'd only meant to kiss her, to acknowledge the bond they shared, both having been abandoned by their mothers when they were young, both still struggling with unanswered questions. Emma's response to that first kiss had been so honest, so open, that it knocked him sideways. After he had tasted her mouth and felt it yield to him, the hazy part of his brain that still functioned had tried to slow things down, to give her the chance to change her mind. Instead she'd stepped back into his arms, her eyes dark with desire and her lips softly parted. By the time he realized she was a virgin, it was way too late to stop.

Now he figured the talk they should have had afterward was eight months overdue. And he still had no idea what to say to her.

First he had some fence to mend, as the locals would put it, but challenges didn't concern him. Nothing came easy in this life and he'd always gone after what he wanted. Some people accused him of being ruthless; he called it persistence.

Brandon grabbed the roses he'd bought on impulse and followed a group of people toward the café. When he glimpsed Emma through the window, a jolt of desire went through him. Time hadn't embroidered her image in his mind. With her long auburn hair pulled back into some kind of smooth knot, exposing her rounded chin and the curve of her neck, she looked both warmly familiar and yet different in a way he couldn't quite pinpoint. His grip tightened on the flowers. He'd been a fool to neglect her for so long, but Brandon Harper rarely made the same mistake twice.

From inside the café, Emma glanced at the large party coming through the front door as she headed back to the kitchen. She was going on a much-needed break; let the other waitresses deal with the newcomers.

Pouring herself a cup of coffee, she sank gratefully down at a small table half hidden by stacks of cartons and put her tired feet up on an empty chair. Not for the first time, she wondered what she was still doing in Whitehorn now that her reason for coming here had blown up in her face like an M-80 with a defective fuse.

It had taken Emma months to trace her birth mother, and weeks more to deal with the news that the meeting Emma had so looked forward to would have to take place at the nearby women's prison. As hard as the truth had been to accept, she'd come too far to leave Montana without finishing what she'd started.

Emma could still remember how nervous she had been when she'd gone to meet Lexine Baxter. Emma had never even seen the inside of a jail before that day and the only citation she'd ever received was for a defective taillight.

At the prison, she was processed and shown to the visitors' room. Part of her wanted to bolt, fantasies intact, but her curiosity and her need for answers were too strong. Finally a guard brought in an older woman who sat on the other side of the Plexiglas window.

Emma had been so busy staring that she nearly forgot to pick up the phone. She could see no family resemblance in her mother's face, etched in bitter lines, nor the brassy hair, grown out at the roots, nor the flat, hard gaze that bored into hers.

The woman was nothing like the parent Emma had prayed would rescue her from each new foster home in which she'd been dumped, alone and scared. Face-to-face with reality, she struggled to keep an open mind.

At first Lexine seemed pleased to see her, but her attitude shifted when Emma asked how she could have abandoned her own baby. Instead of taking responsibility, Lexine piled one excuse on top of another. She'd gotten mixed up with a married man, had to scramble for work, become involved with the wrong people, had bad breaks, believed Emma was better off without her. She was so intent on painting herself as a victim that she even blamed the men she killed for provoking her.

The lack of sympathy Emma hadn't bothered to hide sent Lexine into a rage, the abrupt change in her a shock to witness. She accused Emma of looking for her because she might have money hidden away. Considering Lexine Baxter's present circumstances, the idea was ludicrous. The sheer unfairness of the accusation brought tears to Emma's eyes, and Lexine's scathing remarks about Emma's appearance broke her heart.

Finally she'd run from the room in tears with the sound of Lexine's harsh laughter echoing in her ears. Just thinking about it still made Emma want to cry.

For so many years she had dreamed of finding her birth mother. Now Emma felt as though she'd been rejected for a second time; she was drifting, unable to make plans, unwilling to move on. Except for the couple who raised her, there was nothing left for her back in South Dakota; at least here she had a job, a few friends, and a roof over her head.

She moved to push her glasses back up and then remembered that she'd replaced them with contact lenses a couple of weeks before. Lexine's cruel comments about her appearance had been a factor in her decision, but Emma was pleased with the change and she'd gotten several compliments at work. As far as she was concerned, her improved appearance was the only good thing to come from the whole painful incident.

The confrontation with Lexine wasn't the only reason Emma would never forget this little Montana town. For a while Brandon Harper had played a big part in her reluctance to leave, until it became painfully obvious that what had been a turning point in Emma's life had been nothing more than a one-night stand for the wealthy entrepreneur.

If Brandon had been back to Whitehorn since he'd crawled out of her bed, she hadn't seen him. She tried not to think about him and she'd long since given up on the idea that he might contact her.

She sipped her coffee and glanced at the clock. Now that she'd actually met Lexine, who had to be one of the most infamous citizens Whitehorn had ever seen, Emma was thankful she had followed her instinct and not told anyone in town about their relationship. If Emma's luck held, it would stay her secret until she was long gone.

"Emma! Where's Emma?" Charlene, one of the other waitresses, demanded, poking her head through the door. She saw Emma sitting at the table with her feet up. "You better get out here, girl. Someone's here looking for you and he's got flowers."

Emma gaped at the older woman. "Is this another one of your jokes? If you make me get up for nothing,

I'll see that the next party with little kids sits at your station.''

With one finger, Charlene drew a big X on her ample chest. ''Cross my heart. But if you aren't interested, I'll be more than happy to take the roses and the fellow that brung 'em off your hands. He's enough to make a statue drool.''

Curious now, Emma got to her feet. Charlene had to be mistaken. ''What would Will think about that?'' Emma asked. Will was Charlene's boyfriend of a dozen years and a fixture at the counter every morning for breakfast.

Charlene chuckled as Emma brushed past her. ''Who says I'd tell Will?'' she muttered.

Emma took one look at the man seated at his usual table in her section and froze. Brandon Harper! Had her thoughts somehow conjured him up?

She was about to duck back into the kitchen when he glanced up and saw her. He got to his feet and held out a sheaf of yellow roses wrapped in green paper. His smile was every bit as lethal as she remembered, his eyes just as blue. Heat flooding her cheeks, she managed to walk over to his booth without stumbling.

''Hi,'' he said as easily as if it had been days and not months since she'd seen him. As if their last meeting had been here at the Hip Hop and not her tiny apartment. ''How have you been?''

Emma wanted to demand why he even bothered to ask when it was obvious he hadn't given her a thought since he'd slid from her arms like the snake he was and left without a backward glance. Instead of throwing her order pad at his head, she dragged up a return smile and tried to act as though a floral gift from an old lover was an everyday occurrence. Considering that Brandon had been her first, it was a little hard to pull off.

"I'm fine," she replied with a careless toss of her head, ignoring the roses. "Would you like a menu?"

Brandon's expression tightened and he laid down the flowers. "Emma—" he began again.

She glanced around and tapped her order pad with her pencil. Several customers seated at the counter had turned to watch. "I'm busy," she hissed, the heat of embarrassment warming her face. She'd always hated being the center of attention. "Shall I get you a menu or are you ready to order?"

He sighed and sat back down. "I guess you can bring me a menu," he replied, his eyes narrowing as he studied her.

For a moment Brandon's gaze held hers. Emma refused to soften her brittle smile. If she relaxed her features even a little bit, she might just cry instead.

By the time Emma brought his steak sandwich and fries, Brandon's smile was firmly back in place.

"You forgot your flowers," he said after she'd set down his plate with a thump.

Wordlessly she picked up the bouquet as though it were a piece of meat that had turned bad and made a beeline for the kitchen. When she came back with his iced tea, he resisted the temptation to ask whether she'd bothered to smell the roses before chucking them in the garbage. "Can you sit for a minute?" he invited instead, refusing to be discouraged by her unfriendly attitude.

"I just came off my break." There was more ice in her voice than in his drink.

"Take another one," he suggested cavalierly, trying to look at the bright side. At least she wasn't indifferent.

Her response to his suggestion was like the blast of an air conditioner. "Not a chance."

Brandon leaned closer. "I like the new look." He'd realized she wasn't wearing her glasses anymore, that she had contacts now. Of course it wasn't technically new to him; she certainly hadn't been wearing her glasses in bed, but she'd worn them at work.

Her hand went to her face, as if to push the glasses back up her nose. At the last moment she fingered her tiny gold earring instead. "I'm so glad you approve." She glanced around, but her section was empty except for two elderly couples who were talking over sandwiches and coffee.

"So why are you here?" she demanded, a hand on her hip.

He'd been about to tell her that he hadn't been able to get her out of his mind, but her tone of voice struck his ego like a sour note at a symphony. He'd have to work up to it gradually.

"I'm visiting my relatives," he drawled instead, even though he hadn't given the Kincaids a thought until now.

A man's pride could only take so much rejection at one time. He'd brought flowers, which she'd done her best to ignore. He'd been willing to apologize for neglecting her, had she given him the chance. Instead she'd attempted to turn him into a human Popsicle with her icy gaze. Perhaps he needed to rethink the entire situation before he made any more tactical errors.

A young couple sat in a nearby booth, hands clasped across the table. The man was wearing a battered Stetson and scarred boots. Their clothes showed hard wear. Emma glanced over her shoulder, but the couple appeared to be much more interested in each other than in anything the café might have to offer.

Brandon found himself envious of the rapt attention the rather plain woman paid the man as he talked. What would it feel like to be the recipient of such adoring concentration, even when one lacked wealth or power, as it was obvious the other man did? Suddenly Brandon felt a raw emptiness inside he knew the sandwich in front of him would do nothing to fill.

While he was trying to not stare at the other couple, Emma walked away. She took with her Brandon's last hope that roses and a smile might smooth her ruffled feelings so they could pick up where they'd left off back in August.

With a twinge of regret, he recalled the connection to her he'd felt when she talked about growing up in foster homes, as he had, hungering to know her real parents. She'd been sure they had abandoned her because she wasn't good enough, and she was scared that no one would ever love her because she didn't deserve it. He had wanted to tell Emma then that he'd experienced every one of those doubts, but the words stuck in his throat. He thought back to his own foster parents. All of them. Just an infant when he entered the foster care system, Brandon had been quickly adopted by the Harpers, a young childless couple from Nevada. But his adoptive father turned out to be abusive, and at only eight years old, Brandon had been removed from the Harper house and shuffled from one foster home to another. Though as an adult he'd tried telling himself differently—to no avail—as a child, he'd believed deep down inside his heart that it was his own fault that it never worked out with any of those families. He'd never admitted those feelings to anyone, certainly not to other women he knew. Now he was damned glad he hadn't said anything to Emma, either.

She brought him a red squeeze bottle of catsup and slapped it down beside his plate. "Will there be anything else?" she asked with exaggerated politeness.

The face he'd seen glowing with pleasure was now carefully blank. The hair that had brushed his naked skin was tamed, with only a few wisps floating free. The lips that had softened and parted beneath his were compressed into a straight line. Worst of all, the eyes that misted with pleasure were cold.

Brandon glanced down at his sandwich and shook his head. "No, thanks." His appetite had fled.

Emma tore off his check and laid it next to his iced

tea. "I'll be your cashier when you're ready," she recited without feeling.

He watched her walk over to the other table, hips swaying gently, and greet the young couple. Then Brandon turned his attention to the lunch he no longer wanted. Perhaps he would drive on out to the ranch, after all, just so his return to Whitehorn wasn't a total waste of time.

With a sigh of regret, Emma watched the brake lights on Brandon's car flicker as he exited the parking lot. After he'd tossed down some bills and left without trying to talk to her again, she'd given the flowers to Charlene, knowing she couldn't bear to take them home where the golden blooms and waxy dark green leaves would only serve as an unhappy reminder of something that had started so wonderfully and ended up so painfully wrong. Despite the sneer from her sensible side, Emma hadn't been able to resist keeping one perfect bud for herself.

For a moment when she'd first seen Brandon sitting in his habitual place, casually dressed in a gray tweed jacket over jeans and a blue chambray shirt, happiness burst in her chest. Her surroundings faded abruptly and all she could see was him, hair mussed, eyes dark with passion, as he'd been the last time they'd been together. He'd been wearing the same killer smile that night, the one that turned her good sense to mush and her resistance to jelly.

Then reality came rushing back. She felt

so…vulnerable. So out of control, as she had at the prison. It was a helpless feeling.

He'd made her first time into the memory every woman hoped for, and then he'd dropped off the earth without a word. She'd spent the first week jumping when the phone rang, rushing to the mailbox, looking up expectantly every time the door to the café opened to admit a customer. The second week she'd examined everything she'd said and done that night with him, trying to figure out what had gone wrong, and bursting into tears without warning. She'd told Janie that her hormones were giving her fits, but she didn't think Janie bought the excuse.

Finally realization dawned. Brandon had no reason to call. She had opened herself up, both emotionally and physically, but it hadn't been enough to hold his attention. Simply put, she'd bored him, both in and out of bed. That hurt worse than the pain of missing him. Eventually, though, the wound had scabbed over, but now he'd come back to rip it open again.

When Charlene had first summoned her from the kitchen, Emma's survival instincts had risen like the protective shields on an intergalactic starship. Red eyes, sleepless nights and a wastebasket full of tear-soaked tissues were the least of what her bad judgment had already cost her. Between Brandon and her mother, Emma felt as though she'd had more than her share of disappointments since coming to Montana. Caution had been a painful lesson, but one she'd learned well.

"What's going on between you and our resident

hunk?'' Janie asked Emma, making her jump. ''I haven't seen him in months.''

Though Janie and Charlene—and even Melissa North, the café owner—had teased her unmercifully when Brandon had come in over the summer, at least none of them had commented when he disappeared. If Janie or her husband, Reed, had seen Brandon's car the night he stayed at Emma's, they hadn't mentioned it to her. But now that he'd resurfaced, Janie was asking questions, especially when he'd shown up bearing fifty bucks' worth of roses.

''Until today, I hadn't seen him, either,'' Emma replied. ''And there's nothing going on.'' She liked working with Janie, she appreciated the garage apartment the Austins let her rent and she didn't want to appear rude, but she wasn't up for dissecting Brandon's behavior. ''He just came by for lunch.'' She didn't mention the roses, hoping Janie wouldn't, either.

Janie searched Emma's face. ''He's always seemed nice enough, but just remember that men like Brandon play by a whole different set of rules than the good ol' country boys we know and love. Be careful, girlfriend.''

Emma swallowed a laugh. Janie's warning had come a little too late. Emma had learned the hard way how very differently she and Brandon saw the world.

When she didn't reply, Janie pursed her lips. ''Are you okay?''

''I'm fine.'' Emma patted her shoulder. ''Thanks for asking.'' Sometimes Janie acted like a mother hen, even though she was about the same age as Emma. Maybe it came from being married to a deputy sheriff.

Emma glanced toward the kitchen and saw that her order was up. It gave her an escape before Janie could ask any more questions. When Emma grabbed the plates from under the heat lamps, she noticed that Janie was still watching her with a concerned expression. Emma managed a reassuring grin, even though she felt more like sobbing with disappointment over all her broken dreams.

Two

Brandon had parked his car and was walking toward the ranch house when his grandfather came out onto the porch, hands hooked into the pockets of his faded jeans. A battered black Stetson was on his head.

"Well, isn't this a nice surprise," Garrett Kincaid exclaimed with a welcoming smile creasing his weatherworn face. "We didn't know you were coming."

"Neither did I," Brandon replied as he went up the steps and stuck out his hand. "My car just steered itself this way."

Was it his imagination, or was there a hint of amusement in the old man's blue eyes as he clasped Brandon's hand firmly? He'd seen Garrett hug Collin and a couple of Brandon's other half brothers, but Brandon didn't yet feel comfortable with that much familiarity. Perhaps he never would. For years, as he was shuffled from one foster home to another, he'd taught himself to shut down, too dejected from the rejection he'd felt when forced to pack his meager belongings and leave yet another home and another would-be family. Part of him felt like the outsider looking in, but all this family that had been thrust on him took some getting used to.

"Good to see you, no matter why you're here." Garrett led the way inside. "How long can you stick around?"

Brandon shrugged. He hadn't expected Emma to welcome him with open arms, but her chilly reception at the café made him wonder whether he was wasting his time.

"I've got a few days." Brandon didn't want to commit himself in case all this newfound togetherness got on his nerves. Most of the time being a loner was a comfortable fit, one to which he'd never given much thought until now.

When Garrett Kincaid had found out his son Larry had fathered seven illegitimate offspring—private investigator Gina Henderson Remmington was still searching for the seventh—Garrett had determined to buy the ranch and divide it evenly among them. The sale was now being held up by Jordan Baxter's claim that he had first refusal on the property. Since the first time Garrett had summoned all the illegitimate grandsons to the ranch back in the spring, Brandon had visited Whitehorn several times.

"Where's your luggage?" Garrett asked as he led the way to the kitchen, which seemed to be the heart of the house despite a sprawling living room with oversize furniture and a huge fireplace.

"My bag's in the car. I'll get it later." Brandon hadn't brought it in with him because part of him hadn't learned to count on his reception here. The easy way this man he'd known for less than a year accepted Brandon into his family was both amazing and a little scary. Except for a high school football coach who'd taken Brandon under his wing, he'd done pretty damn well for himself without a father figure in his life. He was thirty-three and he wasn't entirely convinced he had any use for one at this late date.

Garrett withdrew two beers from the massive refrigerator. Popping the tops, he handed one to Brandon.

"You know you can bunk here as long as you like," he said. "A couple of the bedrooms are always empty."

That was no surprise; the big old house had seven.

"In fact, I'm going down to the Black Boot with Collin and Wayne later to play some pool. You're welcome to tag along," the old man added after he'd drained a third of his beer in one long swallow and wiped his mouth on the back of his hand.

Since Brandon had struck out with Emma, he was at loose ends for the evening. The noisy, lowbrow atmosphere of the local bar was probably just what he needed to divert his mind from weightier issues for a while.

"Sure," he said, taking a drink. "Count me in."

"I don't know why I let you talk me into this," Emma mumbled, tugging down the hem of her short skirt as she followed the two other single women into the dimly lit bar. Emma's dress seemed to ride up as she walked.

Dark paneling and an array of mounted animal

heads on the walls, their glass eyes wide and staring
through the haze of cigarette smoke, contributed to
the room's cavelike appearance. Neither of the other
women heard Emma's complaint over the honky-tonk
music pouring from the jukebox and the babble of
conversation. Patty worked in the Mini-Mart where
Emma bought her gas and groceries. The Black Boot
wasn't Emma's usual scene, but Patty's invitation to
join her and her friend Denise this evening had caught
her at a weak moment. She'd been on her way home
from work, still upset by Brandon's sudden reappear-
ance and dreading the lonely evening that yawned
before her.

At least now Emma wouldn't have time to think
about Brandon. She was too busy fighting the sudden
wave of self-consciousness that hit her as she followed Patty through the maze of tables and chairs
jammed together on the scarred wooden floor. Emma
glanced longingly at an empty booth in a dark corner,
but Denise chose a table in the middle of the room.
In her short leather skirt and matching vest over a
see-through blouse, she was obviously no shrinking
violet.

It was only after the three of them had sat down
and Denise ordered a pitcher of beer that Emma
glanced around. Three walls were lined with booths,
most of them occupied by men in cowboy hats and
women with big hair. At the bar Emma's eye caught
that of a cowboy with a handlebar mustache, but
when he winked she looked quickly away. She wasn't
used to the easy flirting other women indulged in.

Two couples were dancing in the small open space in front of the glowing jukebox. Beyond them was a pool table surrounded by men with cue sticks. As Emma watched, one bent way over the table, denim straining across his compact rear, and took a shot.

"Nice buns," Patty observed as a waitress thumped a brimming pitcher of beer and three glasses onto the table.

Although Emma would have to agree, she didn't reply to Patty's comment.

"Lots of ranch hands in town tonight," Denise said in a throaty voice as she filled three schooners and handed one to Emma. The lively song on the jukebox ended, to be quickly replaced by a ballad. "I wish that blond hunk sitting at the bar would ask me to dance. I'd love an excuse to get my arms around him."

Both Emma and Patty turned their heads.

"Don't look now!" Denise exclaimed. "He'll see you staring." She sat up straighter, thrusting out her breasts and pushing back her long black hair as Patty giggled and Emma scooted down in her chair.

The other women were clearly on the make. Why had Emma come with them? And why had she worn this dress? Deceptively plain, with skinny straps, the clingy blue fabric hid nothing and the skirt was too short. She'd bought it without trying it on first and had never gotten around to returning it.

When she dared to look again, another man was headed their way. He was big, with a receding hairline and a double chin. She ducked her head and studied her full schooner. From the corner of her eye she saw Denise stiffen.

"Oh, no," she groaned under her breath.

"Would you like to dance?"

Booted feet had stopped next to Emma's chair. Swallowing, she glanced up. And up.

The man was looking at her with a smile that didn't quite mask his anxiety. There were beads of perspiration on his high forehead.

"I—I don't think so," she stammered.

"Oh, go ahead," Patty urged. Denise kicked her under the table and they both snickered.

The man flushed and his smile wavered. He began to retreat. "Uh, thanks anyway."

Two cowboys perched on bar stools had turned to watch the exchange with obvious interest. One elbowed the other and made some remark that elicited a loud guffaw. Emma could imagine the ribbing the poor man was in for when he returned to his place at the bar.

"Wait," she said, pushing back her chair before he could turn away. "I've changed my mind."

His face turned even redder as she managed a smile and got to her feet, but his eyes were friendly. He recovered fast enough to take her hand in his damp paw. Ignoring the stares of her companions, Emma resisted the urge to tug at her skirt.

"I'm Hal," he said, leading her between the tables.

"I'm Emma." She was relieved that no one seemed to be paying them any attention.

There was an awkward moment when they reached

the cleared area where other people were already dancing. Hal held out his arms expectantly and she hesitated, but it was too late for second thoughts. A rejection now would be even more humiliating for him. Cautiously, Emma placed one hand on his shoulder and slipped the other into his. It had been a while since she'd danced with anyone. To her relief, Hal's mechanical movements were easy to follow and he didn't try to hold her too closely.

"I haven't seen you in here before," he said after they'd taken a few steps and Emma began to relax.

"It's my first time," she admitted. When he turned her, she saw Denise plastered up against the blond cowboy with her head tucked against his shoulder and her eyes squeezed shut. Patty was dancing with a man Emma hadn't noticed before.

"Do you come here a lot?" Emma asked Hal.

"Every chance I get. Don't you work at the Hip Hop? I've been in there a few times."

She didn't remember him. Before she could reply, a hand tapped his shoulder.

"Mind if I cut in?"

At the sound of the familiar voice, Emma trod hard on Hal's foot and her head jerked up.

Brandon!

Hal's arm dropped away from her waist, but she had a death grip on his hand. He didn't seem to know what to do.

"Hello, Emma." Brandon shifted around so she was forced to look into his face. Like Hal, he wore no cowboy hat, but any resemblance stopped there.

Brandon was taller and leaner, except for his wide shoulders. He was wearing a black shirt with pearl snaps. His eyes were narrowed and a muscle jumped in his cheek.

"Do you know this guy?" Hal asked bravely.

Emma nodded. "But I don't want to dance with him." It had never occurred to her that she might run into Brandon at a place like the Black Boot. The rundown bar didn't seem to be his style.

Hal swallowed, clearly out of his element. He sent her a pleading look. "He's not your husband, is he?"

"No." Emma wished the song would end so she could go back to the table. Her face went hot at the attention the three of them were getting from the bar's other patrons. Even Denise had opened her eyes to stare curiously.

"Is there a problem?" Two men in Western dress had materialized to align themselves on either side of Brandon. One was holding a pool cue and the other, gray-haired, draped an arm across Brandon's shoulders.

Hal seemed to shrink visibly and his face lost much of its ruddy color. He shook loose of Emma's hand as though it had scorched him, while her embarrassment turned to annoyance. The air was thick with testosterone.

"No problem," Brandon assured his sidekicks with an easy smile. "Go on back to your game."

"You sure?" drawled the one who looked old enough to be his grandfather. Emma wondered if these men were part of the Kincaid family.

"I'm sure. Thanks, Garrett."

After they sauntered away, Hal turned back to Emma, looking as though he would rather be in a pit full of rattlesnakes than here with her. He cleared his throat. "I don't want any trouble."

Brandon leaned closer and gave him one of those man-to-man smiles, ignoring Emma as he might a store mannequin. "She and I had a little misunderstanding, you know?" he told Hal. "I'd really appreciate the chance to talk to her."

"I have nothing to say to him," Emma told Hal, trying to insinuate herself between the two men. Both ignored her. "Tell him to go away."

"Not until I talk to her," Brandon said stubbornly.

Hal's gaze darted back and forth between them like a spectator at an air hockey tournament. The beads of perspiration on his forehead had multiplied.

The ballad on the jukebox had finally ended, but the other couples stayed where they were, either waiting for the next number or hoping for a fight, Emma wasn't sure which. She wanted to tell both men to leave her alone, but anger had a stranglehold on her throat, choking her vocal cords. She was tempted to stamp her foot in sheer frustration, but the way her luck was going she'd sprain her ankle in the flimsy, high-heeled shoes she'd worn.

"How about it, friend?" Brandon asked Hal. "I'd consider it a favor if you'd step aside."

"Sure thing," Hal replied, walking away without another glance at Emma. She wanted to shout after him that he owed her. All she'd been trying to do was to spare *him* from a little razzing by his buddies!

Another slow song started and before she could protest Brandon swept her into his arms. Oh, my, but the man was smooth. She didn't even have to think about what her feet were doing, which was just as well. She was too distracted by the way her senses were reacting to the scent of his cologne, something that whispered success and sex, and to the warmth of his hands on her waist. For the space of a heartbeat she even forgot she was angry with him.

"I've missed you," he murmured in her ear, spoiling the moment.

Emma's head jerked back as though he'd slapped her. "Like you'd miss a bad case of jock itch!"

His stunned expression was priceless. Then he threw back his head and laughed. The other dancers all stared and Emma's face flamed as she stumbled. When she attempted to turn away, his arms imprisoned her. He leaned closer and his warm breath caressed her cheek, making her stiffen to keep herself from melting like hot wax.

"I'm sorry I neglected you," he mouthed into her ear. "I'm a selfish pig."

Emma leaned back in his arms. "How refreshingly honest," she said dryly.

Brandon's lips twitched, but he maintained his earnest expression. "What can I do to make amends?"

She wanted to tell him to leave her alone, but the words wouldn't come. "What do you have in mind?" she found herself asking instead.

His eyes widened in surprise at her apparent capitulation, but he recovered quickly. "Let me think,"
he murmured as he guided her around the small dance
floor.

For several moments he didn't speak while Emma
struggled to remain aloof. Despite her efforts to resist
his charm, she found herself relaxing against him, her
heartbeat speeding up as the blood in her veins thick-
ened and slowed. She sighed as he urged her closer,
his hard thighs brushing hers, his hands caressing her
back in lazy circles. The music swirled around them,
seducing her. A dreamy smile curved her lips and her
eyes drifted shut.

Suddenly she straightened and popped them open.
How could she give in so easily after he'd ignored
her existence for months? Where he was concerned,
it was all too obvious she was dangerously weak.
"Let me go!" she exclaimed.

To her disappointment, he did just that, his arms
dropping away like fallen trees.

She expected to see a persuasive smile on his attractive face. To her bewilderment, he was frowning.

"Damn it, I missed you," he growled, as though
not seeing each other had been *her* fault.

"That's your problem." Emma stuck her nose in
the air and whirled away just as the music ended, but
he snagged her wrist before she could take two steps.
As soon as he'd spun her back around, his grip gen-
tled and shifted. Turning her hand over, he lifted it to
his mouth.

Emma stared at his absurdly thick lashes as the

touch of his lips on the inside of her wrist burst through her senses like a shower of stars. Was he aware of her galloping pulse? She refused to pull away and reveal just how strongly the erotic caress affected her.

"Will you come with me for a late dinner?" he coaxed, lacing his fingers with hers. "We can go anywhere you'd like." Considering the fact that everything in Whitehorn except the Chinese restaurant was probably closed, his offer wasn't nearly as generous as it sounded.

Emma suspected it wasn't a fortune cookie that Brandon was after. Head thrown back, she flicked her gaze to their joined hands. Part of her wanted to accept and to see where the night led, but pride wouldn't allow her to give in—not after the way he'd treated her before. He'd left her heart badly bruised. Given another chance, he might shatter it beyond repair.

"No thanks," she said, congratulating herself silently for the coolness in her voice. Was that disappointment she saw darken the brilliant blue of his eyes, or merely annoyance? She couldn't tell, but surely he deserved a taste of what she had dealt with after he'd left her.

"Another time, then," he said, letting her go as the jukebox started up again.

When Emma turned away, swallowing the *Yes, please* that leaped to her lips and threatened to spill out, she noticed Denise approach him with a big smile. Funny that Emma hadn't noticed until now how big and white the woman's teeth were, like a hungry shark's.

Before she could sink them into Brandon, Emma hurried back to the table. To her surprise, when she sat down, Denise was right behind her.

Denise thumped down into her chair and refilled her glass. "Who's the centerfold?" she asked Emma with a sneer.

"The what?"

Denise tossed back her hair. "The guy you were arguing with. I haven't seen him around before." She took a long swallow of beer. "Since you weren't interested, I asked him to dance." She laughed, but her eyes were hard. "He said he had a pool game to finish. His loss," she added with a shrug. Denise worked at the local health club. She had a spectacular figure and probably wasn't used to rejection from men over the age of ten.

"So who is he?" Patty chimed in, leaning forward with an avid expression. "Where's he been hiding?" Perhaps she planned to take a run at Brandon next. Let her. It was nothing to Emma whom he danced with or anything else.

Reluctantly she told them his name and how she'd met him, but she refused to answer any more questions, pleading ignorance. It wasn't as though she knew a lot of details about him, anyway.

To her relief, a new song began and a line dance was called, bringing her tablemates to their feet. Emma didn't know the steps, so they left her to sip her beer and try not to wonder why Brandon had acted the way he did and what he wanted from her now.

Audra Westwood stared at the telephone, biting her lip. Lexine had insisted that the best way for Audra to divert any possible suspicion from herself in the death of Christina Montgomery was to call in an anonymous tip implicating someone else. Audra didn't know what Lexine had against Emma Stover and she didn't care. She'd never seen the waitress from the café herself, but Emma was a relative newcomer to Whitehorn—meaning she hadn't been born here—and Lexine was confident she'd make a good suspect.

If Audra had just had kept her mouth shut in the first place instead of spilling her guts to Lexine, maybe she wouldn't be having nightmares about joining her behind bars.

"That's never going to happen," Audra vowed out loud, clenching her fists. But what if someone in the sheriff's office recognized her voice? Maybe they taped incoming calls. What if blocking it didn't work and they traced it back here? She'd better use a pay phone, just to be safe. Maybe then she could relax and quit worrying. Even Micky Culver, the worthless auto mechanic she'd been forced to shack up with, said she'd gotten as jumpy as a chicken on a griddle.

She'd punched him when he compared her to a chicken and he'd sulked for an hour. She wasn't skinny, just fashionably thin, even if her appetite had practically disappeared since Christina's body was found. Audra had hoped it would stay hidden in the woods forever.

Micky thought he was so smart, blackmailing her into moving in with him by threatening to tell what he'd seen the night of Christina's death. He didn't know Audra had run into Homer Gilmore, the town idiot, that night, but who would listen to anything Homer said unless Micky backed him up? The idea made Audra's stomach cramp with nerves. She'd have to make damn sure Micky was too distracted to even think about betraying her. Lucky for her the center of Micky's existence didn't lie anywhere near his brain.

Maybe pointing the sheriff at the waitress would buy Audra the time she needed to find the sapphire mine Lexine had told her about. The gems would buy Audra a new start. There were plenty of rich men in Vegas or California who'd treat her real nice for a chance at what she'd been giving Micky for nothing. Once before she'd been cheated out of the kind of life she deserved, when her stepmother had squandered Audra's inheritance, but this time she was determined to have it all.

She stood up and wiped her damp palms down the sides of her tight jeans, going over just what she planned to say to the sheriff. The last time she'd tried to call him, Micky had walked in, scaring her so bad she'd nearly peed her pants. Right now she could hear him outside tinkering with one of his precious junk cars. She'd wait until he left so she could sneak off to a pay phone without arousing his suspicion. If he found out what she was up to, who knew what price he'd demand for his silence this time.

The list of possibilities was truly repulsive.

"Who was that woman you danced with last night?" Collin Kincaid asked Brandon as the two of them rode back to the ranch house for lunch. "The one in the killer blue dress."

The two men had spent the morning checking the fence line along the east boundary and Brandon felt as though the brisk air had finally flushed the effects of stale smoke and cheap whiskey from his brain. Collin was his older half brother, one of their randy father's two legitimate offspring. Collin didn't say a lot and, until now, their conversation had been desultory without the long silences growing awkward.

Brandon shifted in the saddle. It had been his idea to bring the horses instead of the Jeep. On his first visit to Montana, he'd felt totally out of place. After his customary habitat of corporate offices and boardrooms, the ranch and its rustic trappings had been as alien to him as the surface of the moon. With his usual determination, he'd set out to master the traditional skills of horseback riding, fence mending and cattle herding. Somewhere along the line he'd begun to enjoy the whole cowboy scenario. Now whenever he was here, he spent as much time in the saddle as possible.

Collin's question brought up a subject Brandon had been trying to forget—Emma and her latest rejection. Damn, but she had looked good last night, her red-dish-brown hair hanging loose and that excuse for a dress hugging her curves. He'd been torn between staring like a green kid and throwing a coat around her to prevent anyone else from looking.

"Emma's a waitress at the Hip Hop," Brandon said reluctantly. He would have liked to ignore the question, but Collin and their grandfather had been quick to offer their support at the Black Boot last night, even though it hadn't been needed. When Brandon had first shown up, Collin had gone out of his way to make him feel welcome when no one would have blamed Collin for resenting his newfound passel of bastard siblings.

Collin raised his eyebrows. "So you knew her before last night?"

Brandon flushed. Had Collin noticed the way Emma flounced off the minute the number ended? He probably figured that Brandon had hit on her and struck out, which wasn't that far from the truth.

"Yeah, I knew her," he muttered, reluctant to elaborate. He'd never understood men who felt the need to brag about their bedroom exploits. Some things should remain private. Besides, the way he'd treated Emma afterward hadn't exactly been his shining hour in the chivalry department—not that she seemed to be nursing a broken heart. Near as he could tell, she was just plain mad.

Collin braced his crossed arms on his saddlehorn, clearly waiting for Brandon to enlarge on his reply. "She's pretty," Collin commented when he remained silent. "I don't think she's been around all that long."

Brandon remembered that Emma had told him she was searching for her mother and he wondered if she'd had any luck. "I think she said she's from South Dakota," he volunteered. She'd told him a lot more than that, but he knew when to keep a confidence.

"You interested in her?" Collin asked bluntly.

Brandon shrugged. Interested was one way of putting it. "Like you said, she's pretty," he drawled with a grin. "And my blood's as red as the next guy's." Let Collin draw his own conclusions.

To Brandon's relief, he dropped the subject. Jamming his hat tighter onto his head, he gathered up the reins. "Last one back to the house does lunch KP," he shouted right before he urged his mount into a run.

Collin's quarter horse leaped forward, catching Brandon off guard as he swore and gave his gelding its head. "No fair!" he yelled in protest, but the only response besides the pounding of hooves was a whoop of wild laughter.

After a few futile moments, Brandon reined his bay back to a trot. No point in wearing the horse out when it was clear they weren't going to make up for Collin's head start. When it came to business, Brandon was a ruthless competitor but here at the ranch he would rather kick back and figure out where his life was headed than run a race he had no chance of winning.

Was that what his attraction toward Emma was— a race he had no chance of winning? Perhaps he'd better off forgetting all about her. Considering the idea, he reached down to pat his horse's neck. The animal snorted in response and his trot smoothed out as if he'd been waiting for a little appreciation.

Could that be all Emma wanted, as well? Brandon might be able to read a competitor's expression like a hand of cards that had been dealt face-up, but when it came to a woman, he was as clueless as the next guy.

So far his attempts to forget about her had been spectacularly unsuccessful. All he wanted was another chance to show her he wasn't a complete jerk and, if he was going to be brutally honest with himself, a return trip to her bed that wasn't interrupted by a damn business call. Before that happened, he needed to figure out how he was going to breach the barrier she'd erected around herself, as prickly a deterrent as a damned barbed-wire fence.

Working the lunch shift at the café, Emma took a minute to catch her breath between orders. The usual lull after the breakfast rush hadn't materialized this morning and her feet were as tired as last year's clothing fad. She'd gotten home late the night before and slept poorly.

Walking away from Brandon at the Black Boot had been the hardest thing she'd had to do since visiting the prison where Lexine was incarcerated. What Emma had really wanted was to slip her hand into his and follow wherever he chose to lead, whether it was the Chinese restaurant for Beef Chow Yuk and egg rolls or back to her apartment for whatever might have happened between them. Realizing just how vulnerable she still was when it came to Brandon had been the impetus she'd needed to walk away.

So why had she been kicking herself ever since? Today at work her mind kept wandering back to the bar and the way it had felt to be in Brandon's arms again—until Janie had to take her aside.

"Table four didn't get their rolls and table seven is still waiting for their side of fries," the café manager said with a hint of exasperation in her voice. "The woman in the corner booth complained that she asked for a refill on her iced tea and a lemon wedge. Emma, it's not like you to be so inattentive. Are you ill? Is something wrong?"

Just everything. "I'm sorry," Emma replied contritely as she tucked a stray lock of hair behind her ear. "I'll get to them right away." As she hurried off, she made herself a promise to put Brandon Harper as far from her mind as she could. After last night she sure as heck wouldn't have to worry about him bothering her again. No man as attractive and successful as Brandon would tolerate rejection, and Emma had rejected him twice. Now all she had to do was to quit thinking about him.

She had poured the forgotten iced tea, delivered the lemon wedge, served the missing rolls with a dish of butter pats, and was bringing out the side of fries when she heard the bell over the front door tinkle. Emma didn't take the time to look around. She served the fries, pulled a bottle of ketchup from her apron pocket and voiced an apology, but the woman barely glanced up.

Instead she leaned across the booth to her companion. "My, oh, my," she purred, twirling a strand of implausibly shaded blond hair. "Will you look at the hunk who just walked in? If that's not the best-looking man in Montana, I'll eat my parsley."

While Emma waited politely to ask if there was anything else she could bring either customer, the other woman turned her head and leaned around the side of the booth to see what the fuss was about.

"If only I were ten years younger, I'd toss Fred aside like a worn-out sweat sock," she replied when she'd turned back to her friend.

They both laughed gaily as Emma parked a hand on her hip and resisted the urge to tap her foot. Didn't these women realize she had other customers?

"He's coming this way," the blonde observed. "I'll trip him and you hold him down."

The women were still laughing as Emma finally gave in to her own curiosity and looked around. This time Brandon wasn't headed toward his usual table and he wasn't bearing flowers.

Three

"**W**hat time do you get off work?" Brandon asked Emma before she could stammer out a single word. The two women seated in the booth were gaping, and several other customers had turned to stare, as well.

"Two o'clock," Emma murmured, her gaze fixed somewhere around the top button of his striped shirt.

"I'll be waiting." Without another word, he walked away. As the blond woman released a noisy sigh and Emma struggled to ignore his departure, Janie intercepted him with a welcoming smile and a menu.

"May I show you to a seat?" she asked brightly.

Brandon sent Emma a last solemn glance. "No, but thanks anyway," he told Janie. In a moment he was gone, leaving Emma to wonder if she'd been hallucinating.

"Was that your husband?" the blond customer asked.

Slowly Emma shook her head, still staring at the door through which he'd just departed. So much for her theory that rejection would make him lose interest. Apparently the man took it as some sort of challenge.

"No, he's not my husband," Emma replied absently.

"Honey, what are you waiting for?" the customer demanded. "Reel him in!"

Her companion laughed. "Maxine, leave the poor girl alone."

"I'm not, um, we're not—" Emma found herself stuttering.

"But you'd like to," the blonde said knowingly. "You'd better get busy, honey. Men like that don't come along every day."

Emma could scarcely believe she was listening to dating advice from a total stranger in the middle of the café. "Thank you for your comments," she said neutrally as she laid the check on the table. "You can pay the cashier."

Just then a group from two big RVs came pouring in. Helping Janie shove two long tables together, seating everyone, providing water, booster seats and crayons kept Emma from thinking about what had just happened. By the time she'd taken the orders, heated a baby bottle in the microwave and served dessert to another group, Brandon's unofficial fan club was gone. At least the two women had left a decent tip.

After an hour during which the sudden rush finally slowed to a crawl, Janie came over to Emma, who immediately assumed she'd made more mistakes. It would be a miracle if she hadn't; her mind was hardly on her work.

"Brandon is sitting in his car out in the parking

lot,'' Janie said quietly. ''Do you think there's anything wrong?''

''He's waiting for me,'' Emma admitted, surprised that he hadn't gotten discouraged. Apparently his ego was dent-proof.

''I didn't realize,'' Janie said with a playful grin. ''Did you want to leave early?'' Emma's alarm must have shown on her face, because Janie's expression shifted to one of concern. ''Is he bothering you? Should I call the sheriff?''

''No, that's okay.'' Emma hurried to the window and peered outside as Janie followed. She was right; Brandon was sitting in his Lexus. Paperwork was spread over the seat and he was talking on his cell phone. Emma had been torn between wishing he'd leave and hoping he'd stay. She still didn't know which she preferred, but if all he wanted was to sleep with her again he was certainly being persistent. Could it be there was something else on his mind? But what?

''I told Brandon I'd be done at two,'' she said to Janie. ''If he wants to see me, he'll have to wait until then.''

Janie shrugged. ''Okay, if you're sure.'' She glanced around, but the few customers appeared content. ''If you ever need someone to talk to…'' Her voice trailed off.

''Thanks,'' Emma replied sincerely. ''I'll keep your offer in mind.'' She wasn't ready to admit to anyone how easily she'd fallen for Brandon's charm, especially someone like Janie, who was married and appeared to have her life in order. Unlike Emma, who hadn't even managed to figure out her next step.

Doing nothing wasn't getting her anywhere, she realized a few moments later as she dished up salads and soup for an elderly couple who came in nearly every day. Then she sat in the back with half a ham sandwich. Perhaps the time had come to hear what Brandon had to say. At least that would be a start. Once she'd dealt with him she might even be able to decide what to do about Lexine.

By the time Emma had completed her shift, relieved to see the black Lexus still parked outside, and ducked into the rest room to freshen up before she left, the ham sandwich was a hard ball in her stomach and she was having second thoughts. She might even have chickened out and driven away in her green Chevy if Brandon hadn't glanced up when she turned to the sidewalk. While she dithered, he got out of the car and came purposefully toward her as if he could guess she was ready to bolt.

"We need to talk," he said without preliminaries. "I know I owe you an explanation. Are you willing to listen or not?"

He was persistent, she would have to grant him that, but even persistence had its limits. If she kept resisting his overtures, sooner or later he'd give up and she'd be left wondering what might have happened if she'd been braver.

"All right." The moment she voiced her agreement, a great weight seemed to lift off her chest. She chose to view the feeling as a sign she was doing the right thing.

Brandon had no idea what he was going to say to her after he'd apologized again for his neglect. Normally he was pretty adept at thinking on his feet, and he'd had some hazy idea that the right words would come as he needed them. Now that he was with Emma again, remembering how she had felt and tasted when he'd held her, he wondered if he should have memorized a speech.

Her eyes, an intriguing mixture of green and gray, watched him warily. He missed the melting trust he'd seen there before, trust he'd inadvertently trod on with his thoughtlessness. Was that a bridge that could be rebuilt? And why did it matter so much? Those were questions whose answers he hadn't yet worked out.

"Where do you want to go?" Emma asked.

He figured her apartment was out. A restaurant lacked privacy. Then inspiration struck. "Let's take my car," he said. "We'll come back for yours later." That way she couldn't walk out on him before they were done talking.

She folded her arms across her chest, hiding the logo on her T-shirt. "Where are we going? I'll drive myself."

"That's not practical, but you'll be perfectly safe with me, Scout's Honor," he promised. When he was little, he'd been a Cub Scout until he'd been abruptly taken from his adoptive parents and plunged into the foster system at the age of eight. After that he'd been bounced around too much to join anything until he discovered sports.

Emma continued to hesitate, chewing her lip, as he tried to conceal his impatience. He had a reputation in business for ruthlessness, but he wasn't used to having his integrity questioned. Still, he hadn't gotten where he was today by taking the conservative road.

"Emma, if you don't know whether or not you can trust me, I'm wasting my time here. Which is it going to be?"

Her eyes widened at his question. "Let's go." Her immediate capitulation surprised him. He never knew how she was going to react.

When she headed for his car, Brandon caught her arm. He had to ask. "You *do* know that you have no reason to be afraid of me, don't you?"

Her smile was rueful. "Not in the way you mean," she said enigmatically as a carful of noisy teens swerved into the parking lot, stereo blaring.

Brandon would have liked to know exactly what Emma meant, but he wasn't going to push it until he got her safely to the ranch where he hoped the spectacular scenery might mellow her mood.

"Have you had any luck finding your mother?" he asked once they were on the road and headed out of town.

Emma had been silently staring out the side window, her fingers plucking at the hem of her uniform shorts while Brandon did his best to keep his eyes on the road and not the creamy length of her thigh. She turned her head and frowned, her gaze meeting his before skittering away again.

"I'm still looking." She hated lying but she had no choice.

When she didn't elaborate, Brandon tried to draw her out. "Is there anything I can do?" he offered. "I have some business connections back in Nevada. I could—"

She was already shaking her head. "Thanks, but no. I'll find her."

"I hope your reunion, when it comes, is everything you want it to be," he said as he slowed for a turn. And he hoped the mother she found turned out to be more maternal than his had been. Brandon thought about the day he'd received the report from the private investigator he'd hired to find his birth parents. Suddenly the hope he'd harbored all his life was dashed by the reality of who his parents were. Sheila Parker—he still couldn't bring himself to call her his mother—had been a Vegas showgirl, a star wannabe, who'd had a one-night stand with a young Larry Kincaid during one of his frequent gambling sprees. Though she'd given birth to Brandon, she resented how a baby would shackle her star ambitions. Hoping Larry would take the boy off her hands, she contacted him. But all Larry had done was send her on her way—with a check for a hefty sum. Apparently Sheila had kept the money and then promptly dropped off her infant son at a social services office, going on with her career without looking back. A career that went nowhere. Still, Sheila never came looking for the son she'd given away.

Brandon shook himself out of his personal reverie. "Women give up their babies for a lot of different reasons," he forced himself to say, keeping his own story to himself. "Some selfish and some not."

Her eyes glistened. He hadn't meant to make her cry. "I know." Her voice was low as she studied her clasped hands.

Relieved that she didn't ask about his mother, he didn't know what else to say, so he fell silent.

It was a good thing he was preoccupied with his driving, Emma thought. Otherwise he might have read in her expression the bitter disappointment she still felt.

For a moment she considered telling him about Lexine. Unburdening herself to someone would be such a relief. Then she immediately reconsidered. How would Brandon react to the information that he was in the company of the daughter of a multiple murderer who had killed a couple members of his new family? Emma had a pretty good idea.

So far she had kept her relationship to Lexine a deep, dark secret. There was no telling how people would feel about Emma if they knew the truth. She'd had nightmares about her tires getting slashed, being evicted from her apartment, losing her job, and being run out of town by an angry mob after the news leaked out. She wasn't ready for the loathing she might see in Brandon's eyes once he realized the significance of her birth mother's identity.

After Emma had been to see Lexine at the prison, she'd worried that Lexine herself might spread the word, but as far as Emma knew, that hadn't happened. Considering the way their first meeting had ended, there didn't seem to be any point in a return visit. After searching for so long, Emma wasn't quite ready to put Lexine out of her life for good.

As she drove through the outskirts of Whitehorn with Brandon, he managed to dig some change from his jeans' pocket. With one hand on the wheel, he laid several nickels and two dimes on the leather armrest between them.

"What's that for?" Emma demanded, her voice sharper than she had intended it to be.

"Your thoughts," he replied. "The way you were frowning, I figured they had to be worth more than a penny."

She studied his profile, wishing she were able to read his mind and know his intentions. "Where are you taking me?" she asked when she noticed their surroundings.

"We're going to the ranch," he replied. "I thought you might like to look around."

Emma glanced down at her uniform in horror. She'd spilled soup on her T-shirt that morning and the black shorts made her legs look ghostly pale. "I don't want to meet anyone!" she exclaimed. What would his family think?

"Relax. Garrett and Collin have gone to an auction in Bozeman. Leanne and Cade are out of town.

Everyone else is out moving cattle today.'' He glanced at her curiously. "Do you ride?"

Emma shook her head. As had so many little girls, she'd gone through the horse-loving stage, but there hadn't been money for lessons. "'Fraid not."

"This is horse country. If you stick around, you might want to learn." He didn't offer to teach her, but perhaps he didn't figure their relationship would last long enough for that.

"Maybe," she replied doubtfully. Close up, horses were awfully big.

"Back to my original question," he said. "What were you thinking about with such a serious expression on your face?"

"I was wondering how you've been." Her mental fingers were crossed. "That's all."

"I've been spending most of my time on very dull business."

And the rest of it? she wondered with a jealous twinge. Better not to go there. Emma knew he was an investment banker, but wasn't sure exactly what that meant except it was obvious the job paid well. "Your career might not seem dull to me," she remarked. "Why don't you tell me about it?"

"Basically I put groups of people with money to invest with companies that need it. Think of me as a matchmaker. I seem to have a knack for spotting investments with potential."

"Not bad for a boy who came through the foster care system," Emma said lightly, wondering as soon as the words were out whether she should have brought up the subject. He might regret having told her.

He shrugged off her comment. "I've done okay."

"You put yourself through college?" she asked. With the support of the Stovers, she'd earned a teaching degree, but plans to use it had been put on hold while she searched for her birth mother.

"I had help," he replied. "Luckily I was pretty good at sports in high school. One of my coaches encouraged me to pursue an athletic scholarship."

"I doubt your rise to success was anything as simple as you make it sound. You must have worked your tail off." Knowing how far he had come made her wonder what he saw in her. She didn't think she'd mentioned attending college.

"I worked hard enough," he said in reply to her comment, "but I had a few breaks along the way." He glanced at her again. "Not everyone gets those."

Before Emma could figure out whether his remark was aimed at her, he slowed again and turned through an open gate.

"This is it," he said as they drove over a cattle guard and headed down a well-maintained dirt road. "Welcome to what my grandfather envisions as the Kincaid spread."

The first thing Emma saw was a sprawling ranch house. Farther down the road were more buildings, and a windmill. They were surrounded by a sea of grass and an occasional tree. A row of fence posts disappeared into the distance.

"It's huge," she exclaimed as they passed the main

house. "Does your grandfather think the sale will go through?" At the café she'd overheard the gossip about Garrett Kincaid's battle with Jordan Baxter. Both men wanted the ranch, but lately Baxter had been bragging that he had the law on his side. He'd gone so far as to file a lawsuit to block the sale to the Kincaids.

"Garrett isn't used to being crossed when he wants something," Brandon said as they reached a Y in the road and he took the branch that veered away from the outbuildings. "And he wants this ranch."

This road was narrower, little more than two ruts bordered by tall grasses. "Aren't you worried about your paint job?" Emma asked.

Brandon arched a brow. "It's only a car," he drawled as they drove up a hill. "Would you rather we had switched to the Jeep? I thought you might get cold without a jacket." The spring day was sunny, but a breeze stirred the trees.

His thoughtfulness surprised her, and yet it was like him to notice the little things even as he completely missed the bigger ones, like staying in touch with someone after you'd spent the night with her.

"That frown is back," he remarked, brushing her forehead with his thumb as they crested the hill. "Maybe the view will erase it." Without giving her a chance to reply, he shut off the engine and got out of the car.

Emma rolled down her window and waited until he came around to her door. After he'd opened it for her and she'd gotten to her feet, he stood looking down at her so intently that she thought he was going to kiss her.

"You know, you were pretty before," he murmured, "but you're even prettier now."

"Thank you." Her voice was ragged as she stepped around him and walked over to stand between two trees on the edge of the hill. He came up beside her, but he made no move to touch her.

The hill on which they stood was high enough to give her a better view of the ranch spread out below. Brandon pointed out the two-story bunkhouse, the equipment shed and the old barn. A surprising number of black and brown cattle, many with calves, were scattered over the surrounding countryside as far as she could see. The sun was brighter now, its warmth bathing Emma's bare arms even as a breeze lifted her hair with inquisitive fingers.

"It's nice up here," she said, trying to relax and failing utterly. "Even so far away, the house looks enormous."

"You can tell there have been additions over time," Brandon replied. "The place sat vacant for a while, too, until Garrett opened it and fixed it up. It's in pretty good shape now, all seven bedrooms plus."

Emma tried to imagine the interior of a house that big and failed. She wondered if she would ever have the chance to see the inside. It depended on him and what he wanted from her. If he thought she'd be willing to sleep with him whenever he came around, and be ignored the rest of the time, he was cruising for a major disappointment.

"I'll show you through it sometime," he said carelessly, turning to look at her. "Would you like to stretch your legs a little bit or are your feet sore from work?"

Again she noted his thoughtfulness. "Walking sounds like a good idea." Anything to dispel her sudden attack of nerves.

They turned and strolled back past the car, its black surface covered with a fine layer of dust. If Brandon noticed, he didn't act concerned.

"I made a mistake with you," he said when the silence between them threatened to grow awkward.

Emma's stomach dipped alarmingly. Was he going to tell her that he regretted making love to her? No, she realized almost immediately, he wouldn't have been so persistent if that was all he'd wanted to say.

"What do you mean?" she asked as she kept walking. In the shade of the trees, the early spring grass was thinner and softer. Her heart was thudding and she was trying to figure out how to deal with whatever he might tell her.

Brandon gripped her upper arm gently and turned her to face him. "I didn't think I'd miss you, but I did," he said bluntly. "I haven't wanted to be with anyone else since I left you."

The frank admission was the last thing she'd expected to hear. Emma searched his face, but she had no idea what he was thinking. As usual when she was this close to him, she felt the strong pull of attraction, so difficult to ignore. It sucked at her will, her ability to think coherently, at any thought she'd had to resist him.

"I've missed you, too," she whispered.

Immediately his eyes narrowed and his gaze dropped to her mouth. He leaned toward her, but one last burst of defiance propelled her backward as she struggled against the sensual spell being woven around her by his nearness. He straightened abruptly, a blush skating along his cheekbones.

"When I said I missed you, I wasn't kidding." His voice was low and rough. "But I especially missed this." Arms at his sides, he tipped his head again, giving her plenty of time to retreat if that was truly what she wanted. His hungry gaze was locked on hers, the desire that darkened his eyes feeding her own. She hardly noticed that she'd angled her chin in response to his slow descent.

When there was no more than a breath of space between them, he stopped, hovering so tantalizingly close that she nearly moaned with frustration. Then she realized he was leaving the final decision up to her. Boldly, Emma closed the last millimeter herself.

The touch of his lips was firm and dry. Emma's mind fogged as his mouth heated on hers, moving in a dance of seduction that stole her breath. She braced her hands against his chest to steady herself, surprised to feel his heart thudding beneath her palm. Still he didn't lift his arms, but she felt him tremble.

Memories of his lovemaking swirled in her head, hopelessly tangled with the feelings he was raising in her now so very, very effortlessly. A small sound broke loose in her throat as she crowded closer, sliding her hands around his back and easing her soft curves against the hard wall of his chest as she sought his heat.

Desire fisted Brandon's hands at his sides as he struggled with the urge to crush her against him and plunge his tongue deep into her sweet mouth. Slow, he thought. Take it slow.

Only the certainty that he hadn't yet earned back the right to claim her kept him from laying her down in the grass right this minute. That and the very real possibility that she would reject his advances. Ruthlessly, he held himself in check.

Since the beginning of high school, when he had suddenly shot up to his present height and acquired a few muscles, rejection hadn't been a big issue in his life. If a girl didn't return his interest, he moved on with no hard feelings. His unwillingness to do so with Emma made him nervous. Extremely nervous.

As he struggled now to overcome the insistent urge to mate, the iron control he had honed like a weapon through the years began to slowly reassert itself over his more primal instincts.

Through the cloud of sensation enveloping Emma, she became gradually aware of Brandon's withdrawal. Blinking, she realized she was draped over him like a cat on a heating pad. She straightened as a blush seeped into her cheeks. Now—finally—his hands came up to steady her.

"Are you all right?" His voice was raw, as though it had been scraped against something rough.

Until she got her breath back, she could only manage a quick nod of her head. He let her go and turned away, muttering a pungent curse under his breath. With a hand that was not quite steady, he rubbed the back of his neck.

Even as inexperienced as she was, Emma realized that the passion they ignited in each other was quite extraordinary. But for her at least, passion alone wasn't enough. There had to be more. Brandon knew quite a bit about her, but what did she know about him? Not much, starting with why he'd brought her here.

"What's wrong?" he asked with a frown.

Emma searched his face, looking for some to clue what he was feeling, but his expression was carefully shuttered. She suspected it was the same face he wore when he was closing a business deal or holding a winning hand of cards.

"Do you play poker?" she blurted, and then she bit her lip to keep sudden tears at bay.

His frown deepened. "What?" He sounded baffled by her change of subject.

"There's so much I don't know about you." She thought of Lexine. They both had their secrets.

"I'd say we got pretty close back at your place." His tone was dry. "That counts for something."

There was no mistaking his meaning. Fresh heat bathed her cheeks. "It's not enough, not by itself."

He raked a hand through his hair. "If you're afraid I'll disappear again without letting you know, I'm telling you now it won't happen."

"That's not what I'm talking about." Was she pushing him too hard?

"Then what do you want?" he demanded, frowning.

"Time," she said decisively. "I want to get to know you."

"Seems like you know me pretty *intimately* already," he drawled.

Emma ignored his comment. How could she have slept with someone she didn't trust to understand about Lexine?

"Do you honestly think we can go back to square one?" he asked.

"I hope so," she whispered.

While they were talking, dark clouds had boiled up from the west. Now the sun was abruptly blotted out. Brandon looked at the sky.

"It appears we may be in for some rain. Let's head back to town."

Disappointed in his lack of response to her request, Emma followed him glumly back to the Lexus. As he was holding the door for her, the storm broke overhead. Emma scrambled into the car and he hurried around to the driver's side. Fat raindrops pounded the roof and splattered the windshield.

In minutes the dirt road had turned greasy and slick. Emma breathed a sigh of relief when they finally reached the pavement. As they drove back to Whitehorn, windshield wipers on high and the stereo on low, the silence lay between them like a heavy layer of fog. The weather, Emma thought as she stared out the side window, almost exactly matched her mood.

"Are you hungry?" Brandon asked when they reached the outskirts of town. All the way back he'd been thinking over what she'd said. She was right; despite the speed with which they'd first fallen into bed with each other, there were a lot of blanks in their relationship.

He liked the idea of finding out how her mind worked, which movies she favored, what kind of child she'd been, how she felt about politics and sports, what she enjoyed doing on a rainy afternoon. The only drawback was that he assumed she'd expect him to reciprocate. He didn't much like talking about himself; he never had, but he supposed he could give the idea a try.

"I think I'll just go on home," she replied, the first time she'd spoken since they'd driven back through the gates to the ranch.

"Are you sure?" he asked, afraid to push and yet even more unwilling to let her go with nothing resolved between them. "You have to eat. Let's stop at the Mexican place." He glanced at her solemn face. "It would give us a chance to talk."

Emma twisted a strand of her hair. "Like a date?" she asked, a smile trembling at the corners of her mouth. A smile he badly wanted to kiss to see if he could make blossom.

"Yeah," he replied, suddenly curious about what was going on behind the smile. "Like a date."

By the time they'd finished their fajitas and driven to the café where Emma's car was parked, she was feeling much more positive about their chances. True, he hadn't opened up much about himself, but at least he'd asked her questions and listened carefully to her replies. It was a start, one she hadn't really thought he'd be willing to make.

Now he pulled into one of the few empty slots in the busy café parking lot and killed the engine.

"I had a good time," Emma said, unbuckling her seat belt, and then she giggled.

His eyes crinkled into a smile of amusement as she pressed her hand to her mouth. "What?" he asked, sliding his arm across the back of the seat. Over the past hour, whenever she would think they were beginning to relax around each other, he'd look at her in a certain way and awareness would spark between them.

"It seems a little strange that we're on our first date," she explained, blushing.

His brow shot up. "Isn't that what you wanted?" His fingers brushed her hair, sending a shiver of response through her. Despite his lazy manner, being around him was like waiting for a stalking panther to finally spring. Even relaxed as he appeared now, he evoked a sense of danger.

She considered his question with care. "Yes," she said finally. "Thank you." She picked at the hem of her shorts. "I work the breakfast shift tomorrow, but I'll be through after lunch, like today, and then I have the next day off.'' Was she being too forward? Maybe he had other plans.

His gaze shifted away and alarm went through her. Some men liked to take the initiative themselves. She had so much to learn about him.

''What's wrong?'' she asked when he leaned back against the headrest and sighed, his expression pensive.

''I have to go back to Reno tomorrow night,'' he admitted. ''I've got a meeting the next day that I can't postpone.''

He was leaving again! Emma sat bolt upright and reached for the door handle. Before she could touch it, Brandon hit the automatic locks.

''Wait a minute, will you?'' he said as she blinked back the sudden tears that flooded her eyes. She should have known he wouldn't stick around! She smacked the unyielding door with her fist, but the padded leather panel absorbed the blow easily.

''Honey, please,'' Brandon murmured, putting a hand lightly on her shoulder. ''Will you just listen? Please?''

Emma took a deep, steadying breath and kept the tears from falling by sheer force of will. Embarrassment at her overreaction to his statement flooded through her as she faced him. He'd think he was out with an overpossessive psycho. ''What?'' she conceded.

''I'd reschedule if I could, but one of the principals in a big investment deal is leaving for Europe at the end of the week. We'd still have most of tomorrow, though.''

''I have to work until two,'' Emma reminded him, disappointed.

''Before I go, I'll give you my cell phone number in case you want to call me, and I'll be back as soon as I can,'' he offered. ''Or would you rather beat up my car door?'' He raised her balled fist to his mouth and kissed her knuckles. ''Give me a break, sweetheart. This is all new to me, too.''

She doubted that very much—he was too attractive to not have had tons of relationships—but it was sweet of him to pretend he was as inexperienced as she was. ''I'm sorry.'' She hung her head.

He tugged on the hand he was still holding until she looked up at him. ''How sorry?'' he asked with an outrageous gleam in his eyes.

Happiness flooded back into Emma. ''Sorry enough to buy you breakfast at the café in the morning, but not sorry enough to spend the hours in between with you,'' she told him. ''Not just yet. A girl needs her beauty sleep.''

He pretended to be affronted. ''Don't you think I'd let you sleep?''

Emma lowered her lashes. ''I sincerely hope not.''

''Breakfast it is,'' he agreed, sliding his hand around the back of her neck. ''After you tell me how you feel about kissing on the first date.''

Emma leaned closer. ''Only if I'm really, really attracted,'' she whispered right before he covered her lips with his. Although she tried to subdue it, a little flame of hope sprang to life in the general vicinity of her heart.

Four

The next morning, Brandon was enjoying his Belgian waffles with blueberries and whipped cream nearly as much as he enjoyed watching Emma bustle around in her uniform shorts and the T-shirt that clung so intriguingly to her curves. Although he couldn't fault her for wanting to slow down their relationship, he wondered how long he would be able to keep his hands off her. Not that he would pressure her into anything, but it wasn't as though he didn't know what he was missing. He couldn't be faulted for attempting a little harmless persuasion.

"More coffee, sir?" Her smile was sassy as she held up the pot. Her hair was a mass of curls on top of her head that he would have liked to watch tumble from its confinement. Tiny gold stars dangled from her ears.

Brandon slid his half-full mug toward her. "Please." He wondered how she'd react if he told her what he really wanted. Whipping cream wasn't just for breakfast anymore. "Thanks for the meal," he said, ignoring his body's surging response to the direction of his thoughts.

This morning her hazel eyes were more green than gray. It had been late when he'd let her go last night and she'd already been working when he got to the café this morning or he would have kissed her senseless. Now all he could do was to wait for her shift to be over so they could spend a few more hours together before he had to leave for Nevada.

"Would you like anything else?" she asked, expertly clearing away his empty dishes.

Ignoring the responses that leaped to mind, Brandon leaned against the padded seat and patted his flat stomach. "Not if I'm going to come back for lunch before you're done."

"Oh." Clearly he'd startled her. Pleasure softened her lips and danced in her eyes. Her glasses had disguised that spark of mischief, but now her shy flirtatiousness was starting to emerge.

"Breakfast was on me, but you'll have to pay for lunch," she teased. "A waitress's salary only goes so far, you know, so I hope you're a good tipper."

Before Brandon could answer, he heard the bell over the door. He glanced around to see an old man with long gray hair and an untrimmed beard standing in the entry. His shabby clothes hung loosely on his stooped frame and his lips were moving as though he were talking to himself.

"Who's that?" Brandon asked Emma.

"His name is Homer Gilmore. He's Whitehorn's version of a real character," she replied in an undertone. "He comes in every so often when he's not up tramping through the woods, but I haven't seen him in quite a while." She glanced around. "Janie's on her break and Charlene has an order up, so I'd better see to him. He gets agitated if he thinks he's being ignored.''

Brandon watched her hips sway gently as she grabbed a menu on her way to where the old man waited.

''Hello, Homer,'' she said brightly. ''May I show you to a seat?''

For a moment the old man stared at Emma as though he'd seen a ghost. Then he ducked his head and muttered something about aliens under his breath.

''I beg your pardon,'' Emma said as he kept sneaking glances at her.

''I saw aliens in the woods, but Sloan says there are no aliens.'' Homer seemed to be talking to himself. ''An alien with no hair.''

He shook his head, as though he were trying to deny something, while Emma waited uncomfortably. Several people seated at the counter looked around. The low hum of conversation stopped.

Painfully aware of the stares, Emma kept her patience. Everyone knew Homer was odd. ''May I show you to a seat?'' she asked again.

''No aliens,'' he repeated, lifting his head to look her full in the face. Then he pointed a shaking finger at her as he took a shuffling step backwards. ''You!'' he exclaimed in a hoarse voice. ''It must have been you.''

''That's right. I work here,'' Emma explained.

''No-oo,'' he howled, holding up both hands as if to ward her off. ''The woods! The woods, you were,

I saw," he chanted. "Dark, so dark." His eyes were wide with fright and spittle flecked his beard.

As Emma's cheeks went red with embarrassment, Brandon got to his feet and tossed his napkin onto the table. Before he could get to her, the older waitress, Janie, appeared and bustled over.

"Homer, if you don't quiet down, you'll have to leave. Do you understand?" She motioned Emma aside, and Brandon put a protective arm around her. Janie did her best to herd Homer toward the counter, but he ducked around her.

"She did it!" he shouted, pointing again as Brandon shifted in front of Emma. "Killed her. Sloan said no aliens. This one, I saw. I saw." Growing more upset, Homer stamped his foot. "Killed, killed, killed."

Emma was staring, openmouthed with shock as the color drained from her face. As Brandon tried to pull her away, he could feel her tremble. "You're crazy," he told the ranting old fool, prepared to haul him outside if he didn't shut up.

Janie was trying to reason with him. "No, Homer, Emma hasn't killed anyone." The other waitress watched anxiously, glancing at Emma and then back at Homer. By now he had the attention of everyone in the place. Even the cook had come out of the kitchen with a cleaver in one hand and a scowl on his face.

Homer began to sway, his gaze darting around the café. "Yes, yes," he insisted. "Christina. The woods.

She did, she did!'' Again he glared at Emma. ''Murderer!''

''That's enough.'' Speaking firmly, Janie took his arm as two male customers came over to back her up. ''You'll have to leave now, Homer,'' she said, ''or I'll call the sheriff.''

Brandon was prepared to give his assistance, too, but to his relief the old man allowed himself to be escorted out. He had an odd gait, taking short steps as though his ankles were hobbled. Finally he was gone, the bell tinkling incongruously as the door shut behind him.

Emma breathed a thankful sigh as Brandon turned her into his arms to protect her from the curious gazes of the other patrons. ''Are you okay?'' he asked quietly as he patted her back.

''I'm just embarrassed,'' she mumbled into his shoulder.

''Oh, hon, I'm so sorry,'' Janie exclaimed. ''Pay no mind to Homer. You know how he's always spotting space aliens in those woods. No one listens to him.''

''That's right,'' Charlene, the older waitress, echoed. ''He's not quite right in the head, hasn't been for years.''

Emma's smile was wobbly. ''I know. It's okay.'' She looked at Brandon, her eyes bright with unshed tears. ''Thanks.''

''I didn't do anything.'' Frustrated by his inability to spare her the embarrassing scene, he glared at the other two women. "She's taking a break. Could one of you bring her some tea?"

"Good idea. Take as long as you need," Janie replied. "Charlene, why don't you circulate with the coffeepot."

"I'll watch your tables," Charlene offered Emma as Brandon escorted her back to where he'd been sitting and handed her his untouched water glass.

"Was that nut talking about that woman who was missing?" he asked. "I don't know much about it."

Emma took a sip of water. "It's a tragedy. About eight months ago, a woman named Christina Montgomery disappeared. Last November her car was found, and then her body, in a shallow grave."

When Emma set the glass down, her hand shook, spilling a few drops. "I haven't been following the investigation, but I wasn't anywhere near where they found her." Her gaze was beseeching. "Homer couldn't have seen me in those woods."

"Of course not," Brandon replied, covering her hand with his. "You don't have to justify anything to me."

Emma was grateful for his reassurance. She was about to say so when Janie came back with a tray holding a pot of tea and an empty mug. She set them in front of Emma.

"Forget about what Homer said," Janie told her. "He's a kook. No one listens to his wild notions."

Thanking Janie, Emma opened the tea bag and dropped it into the mug.

"Give yourself a few minutes," Janie told her.

"Charlene and I can manage. As soon as they have something new to fill their pea brains, everyone will forget Homer was even here."

Emma managed a smile.

"That's better," Janie said. "Drink your tea." She glanced at Brandon. "Keep her here until she's calmed down."

"I won't let anything happen to her," he replied.

Janie winked at him. "I'm glad to hear it," she told him. "This gal is one of my best waitresses."

"Has that old crackpot bothered you before?" Brandon asked after Janie hurried away. His eyes were dark with concern. Emma remembered how he had rushed over to her the minute Homer had started shouting all those awful things.

"No, but I don't think I've ever actually waited on him," she said. "He usually sits at the counter." His strange way of walking and garbled language had always made her uncomfortable. Then she'd feel guilty for being glad she didn't have to figure out what he wanted.

The bell tinkled again and she looked up quickly, afraid Homer had come back, but it was only a woman and a little girl.

Emma went limp with relief. She'd hated the way everyone stared at her. What on earth had set Homer off in the first place? It was a good thing no one knew about her connection to Lexine or they might jump to conclusions. What a terrifying idea.

The locals must be used to Homer's ranting. No one was paying Emma the slightest bit of attention now. Grateful, she dunked her tea bag up and down in the hot water. When it was ready she took a tentative sip, pleased to note that her hand was steady.

Brandon was watching her with an expression of concern stamped on his face. "If he comes anywhere near you again, call the sheriff," he said bluntly.

Attention from the law was the last thing she wanted. "Oh, that's not necessary. Everyone knows Homer is harmless."

Brandon gripped her free hand. "I don't want you taking any chances. You'd better fill out a report, just to be safe."

Emma contemplated whether his bossy tone bothered her and decided it didn't. "I'll think about your suggestion," she hedged.

He glanced at his watch. "Do you want me to stick around? I told Garrett I'd help with the chores, but I can call him. He'll understand."

She shook her head. "You go ahead. Take as much time as you need."

"If you're sure, maybe I'll skip lunch and come back when you're done instead," he said, his expression torn.

Emma drained her cup and got to her feet. "That's fine. I'll see you later. It's going to get busy pretty soon and I wouldn't be able to visit with you, anyway." Already the lunch crowd was starting to drift in. Thank goodness the scene with Homer hadn't happened when the place was full.

After she had reassured Brandon a couple more times, he finally left. Watching through the window as he walked to the car, she permitted herself a glow of pride. Although he wasn't all bulked up, like some men, it was easy to see from the easy way he moved that he'd been an athlete. It was exciting to know she was going to see him again later.

She was about to go back to work when the sheriff walked in the front door. In his gray uniform and matching Stetson, Rafe Rawlings was a frequent customer and Emma had waited on him several times herself. Janie's husband was one of his deputies.

"Hi, Sheriff," Emma said now with a smile as she passed him. Too bad he hadn't been here sooner. Perhaps he could have stopped Homer from going off on her the way he did.

Sheriff Rawlings didn't return Emma's smile. Instead he glanced around the café before settling his gaze back on hers. "Miss Stover, I'd appreciate it if you'd come by my office so we can talk."

Someone must have told him about Homer.

"I don't want to press charges or anything," she replied, tucking her ticket book into her pocket. "Sure, it was embarrassing, but it's not like he's entirely rational, is it? I mean, he's pretty old and I suppose he's senile, so he didn't really know what he was saying."

Sheriff Rawlings was frowning as though Emma wasn't making any more sense than Homer did with his strange ramblings.

"You don't have to arrest him, do you?" she asked, puzzled. "Because I won't sign a complaint and I'm sure Janie won't, either."

When she finally wound down, the sheriff cleared his throat. "Emma, I just talked to Homer, but there are a couple of things you and I need to clear up. I want you to come over to my office so we can discuss your whereabouts the night Christina Montgomery was murdered."

The sheriff's office was in an old building on Whitehorn's main street. Emma had driven by plenty of times, but she'd never been inside before today. Wordlessly she followed the sheriff up the front steps, gripping the iron handrail for support.

"Come on back to my office," he said as he led the way through the reception area, speaking briefly to a woman seated behind a counter. She glanced at Emma, who had to resist the urge to stop to explain that she wasn't guilty of anything. Of course it wasn't as though everyone who came in here was a criminal. For all the receptionist knew, Emma might be lodging a complaint of some kind. With her head held high, she followed Sheriff Rawlings through a set of swinging doors into a room with several desks, all empty, and another barred door that she presumed led to the jail. Emma shuddered. At least Janie's husband Reed wasn't here. Perhaps she could clear this up and get out of here before he came in and she suffered more embarrassment.

The sheriff led the way to his private office. "Would you like some water or a cup of coffee?" he asked after he'd shown her to a plain wooden chair facing a desk stacked with files. "I can't vouch for the coffee, but the water's pretty good."

She knew he was trying to put her at ease, but ever since he'd mentioned the dead woman's name, Emma had been as tense as a drawn bow. She now wished she'd paid more attention to the gossip at the café. Although she pitied Christina, Emma had shut her ears to the sometimes grisly speculation about her murder.

"No, thanks. I'm fine," Emma said as the sheriff waited expectantly, his hand on the knob.

Nodding, he shut the door and sat in a leather chair that squeaked in protest. Emma tried not to let her nervousness show, but hiding it wasn't easy. What if she couldn't remember clear back to the night in question? After all, it had been eight months ago.

The sheriff opened a manila folder on his desk and picked up a pen. His first few questions were pretty routine, verifying her full name, her age, her address, and when she'd come to town.

"Where are you from?" he asked.

"Clear Brook, South Dakota." She gave him her street address and the names of her foster parents when he asked. "You don't have to contact them, do you?" What would they make of all this? They hadn't approved of her search for her biological mother, anyway. Every time she called, they asked when she was coming home.

"Probably not." His reply was far from reassuring. "And what brought you to Whitehorn?"

The question hung between them. She thought of

Lexine. No way was Emma going to tell him about her connection to a real murderer. Instead she shrugged. "I was just driving through and it looked like a nice place. I saw the Help Wanted sign in the Hip Hop, so I decided to stay for a while." Even to her ears, her explanation sounded weak.

He was already writing on his pad. "I see. Well, we should be able to clear this up pretty quickly," he said. "All we're doing at this point is eliminating names, so would you mind telling me what you were doing in the woods the night Homer saw you?" He looked at Emma expectantly.

"I—I'm sorry," she stammered, "but I haven't been in those woods since I came to Whitehorn. Homer's mistaken."

The sheriff's eyes narrowed. "Are you sure you've *never* been there? Not last summer?"

Emma gulped and nodded. "I'm positive. Why are you setting so much store in what Homer Gilmore says? From what I've heard, he's often confused about what he sees in those woods." Surely the sheriff was aware that Homer claimed to have run into creatures from outer space among the trees.

The sheriff consulted his notes, although Emma suspected it was just for show. "Actually, Homer isn't the only one claiming to have seen you there the same day Christina Montgomery was killed. Someone else did, too."

Emma's mouth dropped open. "That's impossible. Who else would say that?"

"I'm not at liberty to give you that information."

He was watching Emma carefully, making her feel as though she were under a microscope. "If you weren't in the woods that night, where were you?" he asked.

"When was it exactly?"

When Sheriff Rawlings mentioned the specific August date, she didn't have to think about what she'd been doing. Her cheeks burned as she tried to figure out how to answer his question without humiliating herself.

"May I see a calendar?" she asked, stalling for time.

"Sure." He opened a drawer and slid a card across the desk to her. On it were printed all twelve months of the previous year with the name of the local hardware store emblazoned across the top, each letter shaped like a different hand tool. The numbers of the individual dates swam in front of Emma's eyes like tiny black tadpoles as she stared, trying desperately to think. She knew that telling him an outright lie was the worst thing she could do, so she would have to admit to at least part of the truth, but how much?

"I was probably working that day," she said, tapping the calendar with her fingertip. "The Hip Hop was short-staffed last summer."

He leaned forward, resting his folded arms on the desktop. "I'll need for you to account for the entire day and night. What shift were you working?"

"I almost always work either breakfast or lunch, and sometimes both, but I did work a couple of late shifts that month." Her mind raced. "Then I would have gone back to my apartment."

His dark eyes assessed her. "Do you live alone?"

Her head bobbed. "That's right. I rent the studio over Reed Austin's garage."

"Any chance you can figure out if you went somewhere that night after work, or whether anyone saw you? Perhaps Reed or Janie?"

Emma widened her eyes. "Are you kidding? That long ago? This is crazy. I didn't even know Christina Montgomery, except for seeing her in the café once or twice. Besides, I thought Homer himself was a suspect. Maybe he's trying to distract you."

The sheriff glanced down at the folder in front of him. "Homer has been ruled out," he admitted.

"Why?" Emma demanded. "Did he have an alibi?" She needed to go to the library and bone up on the investigation from the back issues of the local weekly. It was impossible that Homer or anyone else could have seen her in the woods. The sheriff was just fishing around.

"I can't discuss the details of an ongoing investigation," he recited as though he were reading from a TelePrompTer screen. "All I can tell you is that we're not considering him at this time."

"What about me?" She hoped he'd deny it, admit he had nothing, and let her go.

He stood and braced his hands on the desktop. "I think there's something you aren't telling me," he said, leaning forward. "If you need time to check out that day, I understand. You can get back to me, but make it soon. Meanwhile I'll verify what hours you were at work."

Emma stared up at him, cold horror sweeping over her as the gravity of her situation finally sank in. It wasn't enough to merely tell him she'd been home in the evening. She needed to prove it. And what if the Austins had seen Brandon's car? Would he be dragged in for questioning? "Do I need an attorney?" she whispered hoarsely. Perhaps she'd made a mistake in even talking to the sheriff without counsel.

"Do you want one?" In the outer office, a phone rang. Someone must have come in, because Emma heard a masculine voice pitched low enough that she couldn't make out the words.

"I don't think so." Where would she get that kind of money, anyway? "Could I have some water now?"

The sheriff got to his feet. "Sure thing."

After he left, shutting the door carefully behind him, Emma rubbed her temples with her fingertips as she wrestled with the desire to clear herself and the reluctance to admit what she'd been doing on the night in question. No doubt the sheriff had heard it all before and nothing shocked him, but that didn't make it any less embarrassing for her. She hated the idea of discussing the private details of her life with a relative stranger.

She was tempted to peek at the open file on his desk, but she didn't want to get caught snooping. Then another humiliating idea popped into her head. If she told the sheriff about Lexine, would Brandon find out?

Before Emma could decide what to do, Sheriff

Rawlings was back with a plastic cup. She thanked him and took a sip.

Still standing, he extracted a small card from his pocket. Was he going to arrest her? The water she'd swallowed threatened to come right back up.

"I think it would be a good idea if I read you your rights," he said as she bit back a cry of alarm. "You have the right…" As he recited the familiar phrases, voice droning, Emma stared blankly. Sheer terror froze the muscles of her throat and dried the inside of her mouth. Today had started out so well. How could this be happening to her?

While she did her best to keep the tears at bay, he finished reading. "Do you understand everything I've said?" he asked again.

"Y-yes," she stammered, shaking all over.

He sat back down across from her and steepled his hands beneath his chin. "Emma, do you realize how serious this is?" he asked. "It's a murder investigation. Someone killed a young woman who had just given birth. That someone didn't want her found. Christina's family has been through a lot of heartache. If I find out later that you've refused to cooperate because you're covering up for someone else or that you're keeping back something that may help us solve this case, the situation will be all the more difficult for you."

"I told you, I wasn't there, not the night Christina disappeared and not any other time, either." Her voice rose with each word.

He ignored her outburst. "Now's the time to talk

to me," he insisted. "Otherwise it could go very badly for you." He waited. When she didn't say anything more, nibbling her lip instead, he sighed and ran a hand through his hair. "Are you still insisting you were alone after work on the night of Christina's murder?"

Emma felt like a rat in a trap. She didn't know what to do and there was no one to ask for advice.

"If I had been with someone that night, would you have to question him?" This was so embarrassing. After all this time she and Brandon had another chance, but how would he feel about being involved in a murder investigation? What would his family think?

"Yes, the man would have to corroborate your story," the sheriff replied. "*Were* you with someone?"

What choice did she have? There was no way they could link her to the crime and she didn't think they could arrest her without evidence. She took a deep breath. "No," she insisted. "I'm sure I was alone."

He looked disappointed. "You're sticking to that?"

"Yes, but I did have a reason for coming to Whitehorn," she admitted. "If I tell you, will you promise to keep it confidential?"

His expression was impassive as he rubbed his jaw with one hand. "I can't make that kind of promise," he said flatly, "but I'll do my best not to reveal the information unless it becomes necessary. That's all I can do."

That would have to be enough. Quickly Emma told him about her search for her birth mother and how it had brought her to Whitehorn. Was she making a terrible mistake, admitting her relationship to a convicted criminal, a multiple murderer? Would he assume she'd inherited the tendency toward violence? She hesitated, wondering again if she should talk to an attorney first or if that would just make her look guilty.

"And have you found your mother?" the sheriff prompted when she remained silent.

Emma swallowed and licked her lips. "Yes. It's Lexine Baxter." To her surprise, except for a slight widening of his eyes, Sheriff Rawlings barely reacted to her startling announcement. "You know who Lexine is, don't you?" she asked.

"Oh, yeah." For the first time he seemed to drop his professional mask. "Lexine and I go way back. Have you talked to her yet?"

How Emma hated to recall her visit to the prison. "I went out to see her, but it didn't go well."

"I'm sorry. That must have been very difficult for you." His expression thawed ever so slightly. "You know I'll have to talk to her about this."

All Emma could do was to hope that word didn't get around. "Of course. Maybe you can understand that I'm just not ready for everyone to know she's my mother."

Something flickered across the sheriff's face, but was gone again before Emma could interpret it. He jotted a note on a pad of paper. "Is there anything else you want to tell me?"

There was no way she was going to bring Brandon into this unless she absolutely had to. Perhaps she could clear it up without telling him.

The phone on the desk rang and she nearly jumped out of her chair. Frowning, the sheriff picked it up.

"Yes?" He listened for a moment, his gaze on Emma. Then he glanced at the closed office door.

"You can't go in there!" Emma heard someone outside say loudly.

As the sheriff hung up the phone and got to his feet, the door flew open and Brandon walked in. He barely glanced at Emma.

"What's going on?" he demanded. "Why is she here?"

"You want me to show him out?" asked a uniformed deputy from the doorway behind him.

"It's okay," the sheriff replied. "Go on."

The other man complied.

"And you would be...?" the sheriff asked Brandon, as calmly as if people burst into his office every day.

Brandon put his hand on Emma's shoulder and smiled down at her reassuringly as she stared back at him, utterly dismayed by his presence. "Janie told me where you'd gone," he said before he redirected his attention to the sheriff. "I don't know what Emma has told you, but I'm the man who was with her the night that woman disappeared."

Five

For the space of a heartbeat, both Emma and the sheriff stared at Brandon, making him wonder if he'd misread the situation entirely. When he'd gotten to the ranch and mentioned old Homer Gilmore's bizarre accusation to Collin, Collin filled him in on everything he remembered about the Montgomery murder. They talked as they rode out to one of the far pastures. When Brandon got back, he found out about Emma. After Homer's outburst, it didn't take a brain surgeon to figure out what the sheriff was after—and to guess that Emma might try to keep his name out of her explanation.

If she had looked as guilty giving it as she did now, she'd be wearing handcuffs.

"Brandon, what are you doing here?" she gasped, breaking the silence that followed his outburst. "How did you find me?"

"Like I said, Janie clued me in." He looked from her pale face to the sheriff, who'd gotten to his feet when Brandon invaded his office and was watching him now with an inscrutable expression.

"Mind telling me your full name and your connection to Miss Stover?" he asked.

"This is Brandon Harper," Emma said quickly.

"He's a customer at the Hip Hop." Her eyes pleaded with Brandon, but he had no intention of following along.

"And he was with you the night of Christina Montgomery's disappearance?" the sheriff asked.

"That's right." It was Brandon's turn to jump in before Emma could answer. The muscles of her shoulder were rigid beneath his hand. She would have to accept his help; there was no way he'd let her face this ordeal alone.

"Are you all right?" he asked quietly as he gave her a reassuring squeeze, aware of the sheriff's scrutiny and not giving a damn.

Emma's nod was jerky. "You shouldn't be here."

"This is exactly where I need to be," he contradicted her sharply.

"I'd appreciate if you'd both refrain from further conversation until after I've talked with Mr. Harper alone," the sheriff told them as he punched a button on the intercom. "Shane, would you come in here for a minute?"

The uniformed deputy who had tried to stop Brandon from barging into the office poked his head back through the doorway. "Yeah, boss?"

"This is Shane McBride. Would you take Miss Stover out and get her some coffee while Mr. Harper and I talk?"

"Sure thing." Deputy McBride looked expectantly at Emma, who clutched her purse as she got to her feet. She must have realized that arguing would be futile, because except for one panicky glance at Brandon, she followed the deputy without protest.

"Okay, Mr. Harper," the sheriff said as soon as the door was once again firmly shut. "Let's hear your explanation of why you came charging into my office like the cavalry."

"First you answer a question for me," Brandon replied. "Is Emma a suspect?"

The other man's gaze didn't waver. "Let's say that I haven't ruled her out yet. Now tell me about the night Christina Montgomery disappeared."

"I've already said I was with Emma that night. After she got off work, we went to her apartment."

The sheriff jotted something on the pad in front of him. "And at what time did you leave Miss Stover's?"

Brandon thought for a moment. "I got a call on my cell phone. It was pretty late, probably after one. I had to leave for Reno, where my business is located."

The sheriff folded his arms on the desktop and leaned forward. "Do you always get business calls in the middle of the night?"

Brandon bit down on his impatience. "I'd switched off the phone. When I turned it back on, there was an urgent message from an associate. I returned his call and learned that I had to get back for a morning meeting, so I left right away and drove back to Reno."

"I see. And did either you or Miss Stover go out of the apartment at any time before then?"

Brandon shook his head. They'd been too busy exploring their mutual passion, but he didn't volunteer that. Surely the sheriff could read between the lines without Brandon spelling it out for him.

"The ranch your grandfather wants to buy isn't far from the area where the body was found. Were you ever in those woods last fall?"

Brandon had a good idea just where the questions were leading. "Whenever I come to Whitehorn, I stay at the ranch and I help with the chores, or I visit Emma at the café. I haven't had time to do any exploring in those woods."

The sheriff's gaze sharpened. "Are you telling me that you didn't go there with Miss Stover at any time during the night in question?"

"That's right." Brandon kept his voice even. "Once we got to her apartment, we stayed put."

"Until approximately one in the morning," the sheriff commented after he'd glanced at his notes.

"Yes," Brandon admitted.

"And you have no idea what Miss Stover did after that? You didn't call her from your car while you were driving back to Vegas?"

"No." Damn, how he wished he could say that he had, and swear she'd been right by her phone.

"Did you call her later in the day?" the sheriff pressed.

Brandon struggled not to squirm in his chair like a kid who'd been caught at something bad. He felt like a louse. "No, I didn't talk to her."

The sheriff appeared to mull over his answer. "You

spent the better part of the night with her, but you didn't call her at all the next day. When exactly was the next time you talked to Miss Stover?''

Nervously, Emma sipped the coffee she didn't want and watched Deputy McBride over the rim of the chipped blue mug. After showing her to an uncomfortable folding chair by his desk, he'd proceeded to ignore her while he worked at a modern-looking computer terminal. Emma strained her ears, hoping to overhear what the sheriff and Brandon were saying, but all she could make out was the drone of their voices.

She knew why Sheriff Rawlings had insisted that she leave. He wanted to get Brandon's statement so he could compare it to hers and perhaps catch Emma in a lie.

And what about Sheriff Rafe Rawlings? Would he keep her confidence about Lexine or might he assume that Brandon already knew? Emma wasn't sure which embarrassed her more, the idea of the sheriff finding out she'd slept with Brandon, or Brandon discovering she was the spawn of a murderer.

Finally the door to the inner office opened and Emma sat up straighter in her chair as both men came out.

''Thanks for coming by,'' the sheriff told Brandon. Brandon didn't look like he'd been worked over, but neither was he smiling.

Renewed regret that he'd become involved in this

sorry mess made Emma drop her gaze and stare at the chipped blue mug in her hands.

The sheriff leaned over and muttered something into the deputy's ear. Then he beckoned to Emma. "Would you come back in my office?"

How she wished she could question Brandon about his interview first.

"Do you want me to get you an attorney?" he asked, scaring her.

"I don't need one. I didn't do anything." Her lips trembled despite her efforts to keep them still. Even when someone was innocent, just being in a place where people were arrested and jailed was pretty damn intimidating.

"I know you didn't, baby." Brandon's gaze was uncharacteristically gentle, but his voice had a steely core. The fanciful image of a knight on a white charger, fiercely protective of his lady, leaped to mind. A visor hid his face, but she knew it was Brandon. How she wished he could sweep her away from all this!

"I just have a couple more questions," the sheriff told her. "They won't take long."

Dismayed, Emma set down her empty mug. She would have thanked the deputy for the coffee, but he was on the phone with his back turned. Before she followed the sheriff into his office, she looked over at Brandon. "Will you wait for me?"

"I'll be up front." Before he went out through the swinging doors, he gave her a quick kiss on the mouth. It was the next best thing to being swept away.

Once Emma was again seated across from the sheriff with her legs crossed and her hands folded neatly on her purse, she would have given a great deal for a look at the notes he was perusing. The silence ticked between them, making her wonder if this was some kind of test to see if she would crack and spill her guts. The only problem with that was, she had nothing to spill.

To keep herself calm, she glanced around his office. On the walls were a round clock, several Wanted posters with curling edges, and a calendar with a colored picture of a real pig dressed in a navy blue police uniform. There was a window, but the view was uninspiring. Resting on a file cabinet behind the desk was a framed photograph of an attractive woman and a little girl. Apparently the sheriff had a family.

"Do you remember what time Brandon Harper left your apartment on the night we discussed?" he asked abruptly.

Emma hated for him to know the details of her personal life, but there was nothing she could do about it now. "No. I was asleep." Would the sheriff assume she'd been worn out from making love, or was he so jaded that thoughts like those didn't enter his mind? His face betrayed only mild curiosity, but still her cheeks burned. "I didn't wake up until around six."

"Did Mr. Harper call you that day?"

Her gaze skittered away from his and her voice was a whisper. "No."

His chair creaked and she looked up to see that he

was leaning forward, his dark eyes narrowed. "You didn't go anywhere after he left that night?"

"I was sleeping," she repeated. "I'd covered the dinner shift the day before. By the time I woke up, it was morning."

He scratched the side of his jaw with his fingertips. "You said you usually work during breakfast or lunch."

"I'd forgotten about that time. I was only scheduled for lunch, but I ended up staying to close up the café. The cook's wife was sick so I volunteered to do it."

Once more he studied her as though he expected her to blurt out some grisly truth. This time she sat back in her chair and waited him out.

"What's your blood type?" he asked.

She had no idea. When she told him that, his expression didn't change. "Would you take a blood test?"

The request stunned her. "W-why?" she asked, fresh fear trickling down her spine.

"It's routine," he said smoothly. "If you agree, I probably won't have to bother you anymore."

Perhaps it would rule her out as a suspect. "Okay." She wasn't crazy about needles, but anything was preferable to more questions.

"You're sure?"

"Absolutely. How soon can we do it?"

"Right away," he replied, getting to his feet. "I'll run you over to the lab. It won't take long."

She thought of Brandon waiting for her out front.

Their time together was ticking away, but she wanted this ugly cloud of suspicion to disappear.

"How soon will we have the results?" she asked.

"Of the typing? Almost immediately. DNA takes longer, but that probably won't be necessary."

Unless she was unlucky enough to have the same blood type as the killer, she realized, swallowing hard. The idea made her knees wobble when she stood, but it was too late to change her mind. The sheriff would wonder what she was hiding. "I'm ready," she said, clutching her purse.

"I'm sorry about all that," Emma said as Brandon drove her back to the café later to retrieve her car. She'd been shocked when the sheriff had confirmed Brandon's blood type on a laminated card he carried in his wallet. That the cloud of suspicion could extend to him hadn't occurred to her until that moment. "At least you've apparently been eliminated as my accomplice."

"Sharing a cell isn't the kind of togetherness I had in mind," he drawled. "Are you hungry?"

Emma shook her head, appetite nonexistent. Although the sheriff hadn't commented on the results of her blood test, he'd asked her not to leave town without telling him. From that Emma inferred that she hadn't yet been cleared. Although she kept telling herself not to worry, she didn't feel like eating.

"When do you have to leave?" she asked. Maybe he was hungry. She didn't want him driving clear back to Nevada on an empty stomach. Or perhaps his remark about togetherness had been a hint about something else.

"I managed to postpone my meeting, so I'm going to stick around for another day or two," he said as he pulled up beside her car and killed the engine. "I hope you don't mind."

Pleasure leaped inside her. "Why?"

A muscled ticked in his jaw as he stared at his hands clutching the wheel. "I want to make sure you're okay."

Although his declaration warmed her, she felt honor-bound to point out that she'd be fine. "I'll be cleared as soon as the DNA results are in."

"That can take weeks," he replied. "In the meantime, I don't want you fretting about it."

Surely he didn't plan to stay until the results came in. "I'm not worried," she said stoutly. "The truth will out."

"Of course it will," he agreed. "We both know where you were that night."

Wrapped around him for most of it. "You do believe I'm innocent, don't you?" She needed his reassurance.

His surprised expression was enough. "Are you asking if I thought you pretended to be asleep when I left and then you sneaked over to the woods in the middle of the night on the slim chance of finding someone to kill for no apparent reason?"

Put that way, it did sound ludicrous. "Pretty farfetched, huh?" she asked.

"As dumb as the idea that we did it together in-

stead of spending the time in bed.'' His words were
blunt, but his touch on her cheek was gentle. When
he pulled her into his arms, she went willingly.

"Thank you,'' she murmured against his chest. "I
can't tell you how much your support means to me.''

"Anyone who knows you will feel the same.'' He
set her away so he could look into her face. "Now
can we talk about something else for a while? Like,
how we're going to spend the rest of the day?''

Happiness burst inside Emma. "Yes, please.''

They ended up going for a drive and stopping for
a pizza, which they took back to Emma's apartment.
She threw together a green salad and they split a wine
cooler that had been in the back of her refrigerator.
If strawberry-kiwi zinger wasn't a beverage that normally caressed Brandon's palate, he didn't comment
on it.

"It's nice you decided to stay an extra day,''
Emma said shyly after they'd consumed most of the
pizza dotted with slices of pepperoni and black olives,
and he was helping her clean up the remnants of their
meal.

As Emma wiped off the table, he drained his glass
and put it in the dishwasher along with their few uten-
sils. Then he came over to where she was standing
and leaned forward with his hands braced on the back
of the chair. His shirt was open at the neck, his thick
hair mussed. Her fingers itched to sift through the
silky strands while she nibbled on his tanned throat.

"Are you okay?'' he asked.

Emma knew he was referring to the incident with the sheriff. "I'm fine," she insisted. "The truth will out," she added with only a little more confidence than she actually felt. This was Whitehorn, Montana, not New York City. Everyone knew everyone else, and from what she'd heard about Sheriff Rawlings, she didn't figure him for the kind of lawman who'd settle for less than the truth just to close a case.

Brandon said, "If you need money for an attorney—"

Emma shook her head. "Thanks for the offer. I appreciate it more than you know, but the DNA test will prove my innocence beyond anyone's doubt. Hiring a lawyer would be a huge waste of money."

"Okay. I know you didn't kill Christina, but if you change your mind about retaining counsel, let me know. I'll talk to Garrett and we'll get you the best criminal attorney in Montana."

Emma thanked him again, but she knew his offer was unnecessary. Besides, she didn't want to involve his family in something that would blow over soon enough.

"I'm glad you decided to give me another chance." Brandon's gaze searched hers, his expression solemn, as he changed the subject abruptly. "That *is* what you're doing, isn't it?"

Was it possible that a man as successful and attractive as he was could suffer the same doubts as other mere mortals? Emma remembered what she knew of his background, which wasn't a great deal. For whatever reason, his mother had decided against keeping him. Once he was old enough to understand, it must have been a serious blow to his self-esteem. Was it possible he hadn't completely worked through the feelings that so often accompanied that kind of rejection?

The idea that Emma might hold, in some small measure, the power to hurt him, or to heal him, was a heady one. It gave balance to her own painful vulnerability where he was concerned.

He appeared to be totally at ease as he waited for her answer, but she was learning to read beyond the confident facade he threw up like a smoke screen. There was a faint tightness to his smile, a slight narrowing of his blue eyes. Tension hummed ever so faintly in the set of his shoulders and the way his hands gripped the chair.

Those little signs gave her the courage to smile flirtatiously and to close the distance between them. As she gazed at him, he straightened abruptly and turned so they were facing each other. She leaned toward him, her body nearly brushing his. Her heart was pounding so hard that she wondered if he could hear it. Her nerve endings were on red alert and her breathing was as shallow as a mountain stream in a drought.

He didn't say a word, but he eyed her carefully. A muscle ticked in his jaw. There was no sound in the apartment except the slow, soft music she'd put on when they'd first come in.

Emma reached up her hands and grasped his collar.

Astonished by her own boldness, she went up on her toes and kissed him.

For the space of a heartbeat he stood frozen, allowing her control of the kiss. Her arms circled his neck, her breasts flattened against the hard muscles of his chest as she crowded closer. A shudder rippled through him and he widened his stance so she was pressed intimately against him, but his mouth remained compliant, his lips parting slightly to tempt her inside. Bravely, Emma traced those firm male lips with the tip of her tongue and then she gave in to temptation.

His reaction to the caress was instantaneous. He gasped, his hands clenching at her waist, and his control shattered. His arms closed around her like steel bands and he nearly lifted her from the floor as his mouth claimed hers in a kiss so hot it threatened to melt her fillings. Conscious thought evaporated as Emma hung on, giving as good as she got.

Sweet heaven, how she had missed him, missed the passion exploding between them.

Way too soon for her, he tore his mouth away to nibble at her closed eyelids, her cheeks, the lobes of her ears and the sensitive area along her jaw. Emma's head fell back and she anchored her fingers in his hair as he continued to taste her. His breath was hot on her skin, his hands shifting from her back to her arms, to the underside of her breasts. When his thumb caressed her nipple, her knees nearly buckled. Helplessly, she clung to him, surrendering to his sensual onslaught.

Returning his attention to her mouth, he drank in her moan of pleasure as he held her face between his hands. She could feel his arousal. Breathlessly, hysterically, she thought of her white knight and his lance.

Brandon's hands released their grip on her jaw. Beyond her tightly closed lids, the room spun and dipped alarmingly around. Had she laughed? She wasn't sure, she only knew she was falling, twirling—

Her eyes flew open and she stared up at him, horrified to think she might have hurt him with an inappropriate giggle. He had lifted her into his arms and he was staring intently at her face. Although the room wasn't overly warm, his complexion was flushed. Emma blinked, confused. Brandon threw back his head and dragged in a tortured breath that expanded his chest and bared his teeth.

"What?" she managed to ask as he leaned down and touched his forehead to hers. His eyes were closed, those sinfully thick lashes lying on his cheeks like a black fringe.

"I'm sorry." His voice was deep, thick, rough as tree bark. Carefully he set her back on her feet. She swayed, but his arms were still around her. Her mind, moments before a white-hot blank, was tripping over itself in its haste. What had gone wrong between them?

"You wanted time," he mumbled, burying his face in her hair. "I'm sorry," he repeated. "I haven't lost control like that since…" He lifted his head. "Hell, I've never been so…" Again his voice trailed off.

"Are you okay?" he finally asked. "Did I, um, hurt you?" Concern furrowed his brow as he looked her up and down.

"I'm fine." Emma peered up at him, tempted to lick his taste from her lips like a cat licking cream. "I'm better than fine." She extended her hand, intending to caress his cheek.

He backed up so quickly he almost tripped, his palms out as though to ward her away. "Oh, no," he cautioned. "That's how this all started in the first place. Maybe you'd better give me a few minutes."

Normally a remark like that would have plunged Emma into a bottomless pit of rejection and humiliation. Instead the flair of panic in Brandon's eyes filled her with a dose of feminine satisfaction that was as heady as it was new. He wanted her!

As quickly as the surge of triumph appeared, it faded again. For Emma, wanting was no longer enough. She had feelings for him, feelings she hadn't yet sorted through. With a quiver of dismay, she realized that the desire sizzling in her blood whenever she thought of him was only one small part of the total package. She was in real trouble here.

"You look like you just saw a ghost." Brandon's tone was flat. "Did I scare you?"

Emma blinked and then she noticed the dull flush that darkened his cheeks, the self-deprecating twist to his mouth. "Oh, no. Of course not." She managed a smile. "I was the one coming on to you, remember?" As an attempt to make him feel better, the reminder was weak, but it seemed to do the trick.

The harsh set to his features thawed slightly. "Yeah, you did, didn't you?" He looked bemused and then he sobered. "Perhaps I'd better leave."

"Why?" she asked, disappointment wiping away her smile. Had he no interest in her except the most obvious?

Without giving Emma an answer, Brandon wandered restlessly to the living-room window with his earlier lapse of control still heavy on his mind. Before he'd met her, he would have insisted that as much as he enjoyed feminine companionship, it was hardly a priority. The sophisticated career women he spent time with understood the rules; they felt the same way about relationships as he did. Passions were aroused, recognized, acted on and sated without a lot of messy emotions to complicate the situation.

With Emma the rules had somehow been tossed out the window the night he realized she was a virgin, too late to keep from irreparably altering that status, and now he had no clear idea how to act around her. He only knew that when he'd found out the sheriff had hauled her away, Brandon hadn't been able to get to her fast enough.

He was still trying to regain his emotional balance when Emma joined him at the window. He hadn't given her a reason why his departure might be for the best. How would he tell her that if he stayed, he was afraid they'd end up in bed again and he wasn't sure that was a good idea?

His body, on the other hand, had no doubts at all.

"Do you want to watch television?" she asked. "We could see what's on."

Brandon realized that running away from her wasn't going to give him any answers. He turned and looked into her eyes, more green that gray in the waning light. "I've got a better idea," he said, trapped by the war between his conscience and his libido. "Let's rent a couple of movies. I saw a video store right down the street." Maybe something with explosions and mayhem would distract him from the persistent idea of soft sighs and tangled sheets.

Her smile was all the reward he needed. Other people's happiness had never been a big concern of his, although he didn't go out of his way to hurt anyone unless they tried to cheat him. For the first time he understood the genuine enjoyment a person could take from giving pleasure to someone who mattered.

The realization did little to alleviate the uneasiness that was already churning through him like floodwater through a broken dike. Nervously he jiggled the car keys in his pocket, wondering how someone who'd faced down every threat of financial disaster imaginable without breaking a sweat could be so intimidated by one small woman.

"So who do you like better?" he asked her. "Van Damme, Willis, or Schwarzenegger?"

Six

Emma sat next to Brandon on her couch, his arm around her and a bowl of popcorn resting on her lap. His feet were propped on the corner of the coffee table and a laughably bad rented movie played on the television. Every few minutes Brandon would look at Emma and smile, or their hands would touch when they both reached for more popcorn at the same time, sending a tingle up her arm.

She kept sneaking sidelong glances at him, wondering what he was thinking. Earlier when they'd gone for a ride, he'd asked her more about her childhood. After she'd rattled on about the Stovers and how they'd wanted to adopt her but were unable to obtain permission, she turned the tables. Although Brandon hadn't been nearly as forthcoming, he did admit to hiring a private investigator to track down his birth mother. Once she had been located, he never contacted her. When Emma asked why, his expression closed up and he shrugged.

"I found out what I wanted to know," was all he'd say.

Sensing that her questions were making him uncomfortable, she'd backed off for the moment and gotten him talking about his travels instead.

After college he'd been all over the world and the stories he told were fascinating. From what he said, Emma realized he was more comfortable as an observer than a participant. She wondered if that was always true of him, or just when he was in unfamiliar territory. Maybe someday she'd ask, but right now she didn't want to disrupt the companionable mood between them with intrusive questions.

Was that the real reason he'd dropped out of her life before, because the closeness they'd shared was some kind of uncharted emotional territory for him? Nibbling on a handful of popcorn, she mulled that idea over. Perhaps Brandon was the one who needed time—and patience—even more than she did. The question was, could she give him that without becoming hopelessly, painfully tangled in her own loving net?

Emma had no answers. Instead of pursuing the thoughts circling her brain like hamsters in an exercise wheel, she focused her attention on the movie. A few minutes later, both she and Brandon groaned out loud at a particularly awkward line mouthed by one of the actors.

Brandon hit the pause button on the remote and set the bowl of popcorn on the table. "This movie sucks."

Emma couldn't help but laugh. "I'm glad you said that. I was beginning to have grave doubts about your taste."

He narrowed his eyes, but he couldn't hide their

playful glint. "Is that right?" he murmured. "How about my taste in women?"

"That I like," she replied, her voice husky as she ran a hand up his arm. Feeling the muscles quiver beneath her palm gave her the courage to lean even closer. One thing her visit to the sheriff's office had done was to remind her how quickly a person's life could change. Even though the search for Emma's mother hadn't turned out the way she'd hoped didn't mean she had to stop taking chances on life.

"Would you like to stay?" she asked Brandon.

His reaction was all the reassurance she needed that he'd taken nothing for granted. For a moment he studied her face so intently she thought he must be memorizing each feature. Then he lifted her hand to his lips and turned it over gently to press a kiss into her palm.

"I'd like to stay with you more than anything," he whispered, his breath tickling her sensitive skin and making her fingers curl in reaction.

"Okay," she managed to utter as a ribbon of desire swirled through her. This was right, it was necessary. She needed him and she was good for him. Perhaps those icy barriers he'd erected around his heart could only be thawed by passion before love could seek entrance.

It was a risk she had to take.

Brandon cupped her face in his hands and stared into her eyes. "You won't be sorry," he vowed.

She hoped he was right. Her pulse kicked up a gear as his head lowered and she gave herself up to the touch of his mouth as passion exploded inside her. The past eight months without him had been an eternity. Now she was ready to accept whatever he was able to give in exchange for her heart, and to trust that somehow the trade would be a fair one.

Emma's response melted the last shreds of Brandon's resolve. With a groan he deepened the kiss. Slow was no longer an option; gentle and easy were slipping from his grasp as he felt her stir against him in wordless invitation. Desire fogged his brain and filled his groin. No one fired his blood the way Emma did.

His first impulse was to rush her into bed, giving her no time for second thoughts. Before he could grab at his shaky control, she nibbled on his lip, sending a new blast of hunger roaring through him like a giant fireball. He pressed his hand to her breast, brushing her nipple with his thumb and feeling it bead through her clothes. Her nimble fingers tugged at the tail of his shirt, pulling it free to skate her hands up his ribs. Her unexpected assertedness turned the heat up several degrees.

In a blink they were stretched out together on the couch. It was a narrow fit and he nearly rolled off.

"Wait," he gasped as she tugged at the snaps on his shirt.

"No."

Her busy hands were addling his senses, but he nearly laughed at her blunt refusal. Finally he captured her wrists, kissing the fingers that still bore traces of butter and salt from the popcorn. He ran his tongue over her fingertips and felt her tremble.

"Let me pull out the bed, before I end up on the floor," he pleaded.

She blinked, clearing the mist from her eyes, and her cheeks turned pink as she scooted to her feet. "I can't believe I'm acting like this."

Brandon rose beside her and swept together the last crumbs of his self-control. "Is this truly what you want?" He'd die on the spot if she stopped now, but he had to be sure. Hustling her into the sack might be what his body screamed for, but that kind of move wasn't his style. He wanted her crystal-clear on what she was doing, no rush and no regrets.

"Emma?" he asked again, spirits sinking. Damn, was she calling his bluff?

She took a deep breath, then her hands went to the front clasp of her bra and freed it, revealing her pretty breasts. His mouth watered at the sight. Was this her way of getting even after he'd ignored her for so long, taunting him with what he gave up? He watched with the breath wedged in his throat as she shimmied out of her black shorts. She was standing in lacy, high-cut panties and nothing else. His erection strained at his jeans and still he waited as she hooked her thumbs into the waistband of the silken scrap that stood between him and the soul-stirring satisfaction he hadn't been able to put out of his mind. The sweet oblivion he'd never found with anyone except Emma.

"Let me help you with those," he offered when she didn't immediately slip off the panties.

Her smile was soft and womanly. "First unfold the bed."

This time when Emma woke, he was still there beside her, his dark head resting on the pillow and one brawny arm thrown across her waist as though he wanted to keep her close. He wasn't a peaceful sleeper; the sheets were as tangled as if a battle had been fought. Even as she watched him, he stirred and groaned, his thick lashes fluttering. His hand twitched, touched her skin and stilled as though her presence had banished whatever nightmare gripped him.

Her gaze wandered over his bare, sleek shoulders as she debated trying to rise without waking him. When she looked at his face, a narrow strip of blue stared back through the thicket of his lashes.

"Good morning." His voice was rusty with sleep, something they'd hadn't gotten much of, between the times throughout the night that she'd wakened to his urgent hunger and once, later yet, to his lazy, drugging caress.

Now he leaned over and kissed her, his mouth lingering, coaxing hers to moist, pliant heat. As quick as that, she wanted him again. He saw it in her eyes and he complied, sweetly, savagely, with a desperation that told her better than words how much he needed her.

When she woke again, the bed and the room were empty. Swallowing a moan of despair, she scrambled to her feet, still naked. He must have heard her stir, because he appeared in the doorway of the tiny kitchen. His hair was neatly combed, but his shirt hung open, his pants were unsnapped and he held a coffee mug in one hand.

Suddenly shy, Emma grabbed the first thing she could find, her uniform shirt, and held it in front of her.

"What's wrong?" he asked.

"I thought you'd left." The words popped out before she could stop them.

Frowning with displeasure, he crossed the room and caught her up in his arms. "I told you I wouldn't do that again," he said fiercely, burying his face in her hair as he held her.

The tension drained out of Emma, leaving her limp and compliant. Wordlessly she hung on to him, her shirt caught between them. What would he do if she told him she loved him?

How could she love him and not trust him with the truth about Lexine? The dilemma was like a snake biting its own tail; it had no beginning and no end. It just went around and around in her head.

"I'd better get dressed," she said. "Are you hungry? I'll fix breakfast as soon as I shower."

"I'll take you out," he offered, letting her go.

"Thanks, but cooking is a treat for me. Going to a restaurant for breakfast is too much like work. Next thing you know, I'll be pouring coffee refills for everyone." She hoped there was something in the fridge she could turn into a meal.

"While you're in the shower I'll call out to the ranch and see what's up." He reached for his cell phone. "Then I'll help you with this strange custom you call cooking."

He must eat out a lot. Emma returned his smile before grabbing clean underwear from the bureau and ducking into the bathroom, painfully aware of her bare backside. His low wolf whistle made her chuckle as she slammed the door behind her.

A few moments later she was drying off and humming happily under her breath when her phone rang.

"Do you want me to answer that?" Brandon called from the other side of the bathroom door.

Emma glanced at her watch. It might be her parents. Although the hour was still early to be entertaining male visitors, she knew they wouldn't ask any embarrassing questions. What they might think was another matter, but that couldn't be helped. She was a big girl now, entitled to make her own decisions.

"Please do," she replied, trusting Brandon to be discreet about her actual whereabouts. While she listened to his deep voice, she hurried into her underwear. Before she could slide into her jeans, he knocked softly on the door.

"It's for you."

The absurdity of the remark made her smile as she pulled a pink T-shirt over her head and opened the door as she shook out her hair. Her intention was to ask who he'd expected the call to be for, and then she saw his grim expression.

"It's the sheriff," he said in an undertone as he held out the receiver.

Gingerly, Emma took it from his hand and held it

to her ear as cold chills rippled down her spine. "This is Emma."

"I know you probably can't comment, but I wanted you to know that I'm on my way to the women's prison to talk to Lexine," he said after he'd identified himself.

Emma's gaze flew to Brandon's face. Could he hear what Sheriff Rawlings was saying? As though Brandon could read her mind, he held up his empty cup and pointed to the kitchen.

As soon as he'd walked away, she demanded in a low, angry voice, "Why do you have to do that?"

The sheriff sighed. "I can't go into it, but I thought there might be something else you wanted to say before I talk to her. I didn't mean to interrupt anything," he added pointedly.

Emma's cheeks burned. "You didn't," she snapped without thinking. "I discussed that situation with you already and I have nothing to add." She was about to hang up when he spoke again.

"I'm not the enemy, Emma. As long as you aren't hiding anything, you don't have to worry."

"I already told you, I didn't do it." Emma rubbed her temple, wondering what excuse she could give Brandon for the call. She supposed it was considerate of the sheriff to let her know about Lexine. Before she could thank him, he said goodbye and hung up.

As she replaced the receiver, Brandon stuck his head around the corner, making her wonder how closely he'd been tracking the conversation. "Want some coffee?"

"Sure, thanks." She was relieved when he didn't ask about the sheriff. Instead he curved one arm around her and rested his cheek on her hair.

"Are you okay?" he asked.

Emma gulped, longing to confide in him but still not willing to risk seeing the interest in his eyes replaced by pity, distaste or loathing. "Yes, I'm fine," she replied as she pulled away. "I thought you said something about coffee."

His mouth tightened briefly, but then he smiled and she wondered whether she'd been seeing things that weren't there. "Cream and sweetener, right?" he asked.

Pleased that he remembered, she nodded and then she opened the door of the refrigerator. It wouldn't be the fanciest breakfast served up in Whitehorn this morning, but at least she could offer him hash browns made from a leftover boiled potato, eggs, and a bran muffin, along with a grapefruit that was only starting to shrivel.

He came up behind her and peered over her shoulder into the fridge. "It's better stocked than mine back in Reno," he commented, "but that's not saying much."

"What's your place like?" she asked as she got out the breakfast fixings.

He seemed reluctant to answer her question. Tired of his reticence, she thumped the food down onto the counter. "Forget I asked."

She'd spun away when his hand closed on her upper arm. She stopped, but she didn't look at him.

"I'm sorry," he said into her ear. "I guess I'm not used to anyone being interested enough to ask."

Relenting, Emma turned to face him. "I want to hear anything you care to tell me. There's a lot I don't know about you. It's like you drop into town and then you disappear again, as though I've conjured you up. You know where I work. You've seen my apartment." She made a sweeping gesture with her hand. "I'm just trying to fill in a few blanks, that's all. If you don't want to tell me, that's your choice."

"I do," he said, rubbing his hand over his face. He hadn't shaved, of course, and the shadow along his jaw made him look dangerous and very, very sexy. "My house is on the edge of town in a nice area. I guess it's too big for one person, but I bought it partly for an investment. It's white stucco with a blue tile roof. There's a fountain out front in the middle of a circular driveway. I have a pool out back and a tennis court."

"Do you play?" she asked, trying to picture him in white shorts.

"Not that much. When I have the time, I prefer golf or a good game of basketball."

Emma had started fiddling with breakfast preparations while he was talking. "It sounds nice." And very, very expensive.

"I'd like to show it to you sometime."

Her shoulders slumped. "The sheriff *requested* that I not leave the area." She tried to keep the sarcastic edge from her voice and failed. Even cloaked in polite terms, she knew an order when she heard one.

"We'll go after this is cleared up," Brandon declared. "Have you ever been to Nevada?"

Cracking eggs into a bowl, Emma shook her head. Once the Stovers had taken her in, she'd never ventured out of Clear Springs until she left for college. The neon world of Reno was beyond her experience.

"You'll love it. Reno is unlike any other city in the world," he enthused. "We'll have a blast."

It was the promise of more time with him that snagged Emma's excitement. "Sounds fun," she said calmly, even though her insides were jumping, "but don't you think we should eat first?"

Her quip earned her a grin and a quick kiss. "When I'm around you, I don't need food," he murmured in a deep voice.

Emma rolled her eyes and smacked him with the kitchen towel. "Here." She handed him the potato and a paring knife. "Slice it thin. When you're done, you can grate some cheese."

"Ah," he sighed dramatically. "Foreplay."

Emma ignored him, but she was secretly pleased by his playfulness. It was a side to his personality he hadn't revealed to her before. Maybe his willingness to do so now meant he realized their relationship had more going for it than just sex. Emma hoped so.

Audra hated coming to the prison to visit Lexine nearly as much as she hated sleeping with Micky. She didn't know which was worse, feeling his hands on her when he was awake or listening to his snoring when he wasn't.

Lexine had left a message that she wanted to see Audra right away. She knew better than to ignore her mother's summons. While she waited for Lexine to appear on the other side of the glass partition, she picked at the polish on her thumbnail, ruining a ten-dollar manicure, and tried not to think about how badly she wanted a cigarette. There was a pack in her purse she could hardly wait to open the minute she got back outside.

"Did you bring my smokes?" was the first thing Lexine asked after she had sat down opposite Audra and they'd both picked up their phone receivers.

No "Hi, how ya been?" and no "Thanks for coming," Audra thought. Never mind "You look good" or "I like your new earrings."

Lexine's hair, she saw, was freshly styled and tinted a brighter blond than Audra's, temporarily hiding the gray roots that usually framed Lexine's face. Even though she patted the brassy locks with her free hand, Audra pretended not to notice.

"Yes, I left two cartons at the desk," she replied in as sullen a tone as she dared. "And I made that call, too."

Lexine glanced around and then she lowered her voice. "Has she been arrested yet?"

Audra shrugged. "How should I know? Do I look like I've got a pipeline to the sheriff's office?" Micky was getting on her nerves, she still hadn't found the sapphire mine that was going to buy her ticket out of Montana and Lexine's demands were a big pain. Life sucked.

Across from her, Lexine narrowed her eyes. They were ringed with black liner, her lashes caked with the mascara Audra had brought her the last time she'd visited. Lexine hadn't seen fit to thank her for that, either. All she'd ever given Audra was a gold locket she'd managed to lose in the woods. When Lexine had noticed she wasn't wearing it, she'd lied and said she was having the chain fixed.

"Are you trying to be smart with me, girl?" Lexine demanded. "I asked you a question and I want an answer."

Audra's resentment must have shown on her face, because Lexine instantly changed tactics. "We're doing this for you, sweetie." Her voice had gone all syrupy, her expression pleading. "Now please fill Mama in on what's been happening."

Damn, but Audra wished she'd never confided in Lexine. What had she been thinking to give her this much power? "I haven't heard anything."

Lexine rolled her eyes, her jaws working on the gum she was chewing. "Couldn't you call and *ask?*"

Audra hated it when Lexine talked down to her. "They might recognize my voice if I call again," she said with a sniff. "Besides, it would be all over the news if anyone got arrested. Finding that woman's body has been the biggest thing to hit Whitehorn since, well, since you were convicted." She hadn't been able to resist that little dig, even though Lexine's cheeks turned all red and blotchy. A thrill of fear shivered through Audra and her fingers tightened on the receiver as she reminded herself not to overdo it.

As long as Lexine needed her to search for the sapphire mine and run errands, Audra figured she was safe. By the time Lexine realized she had no intentions of sharing the mine's bounty, Audra would be well on the way to her new life and a new identity. Once Emma Stover was convicted of the Montgomery woman's murder, who would listen to the rambling accusations of a lifer? Still, Lexine's temper was unpredictable.

"I'm sorry," Audra murmured, attempting to look suitably contrite. "I'll find out what I can."

"You do that," Lexine replied coldly. "Otherwise I'll have to call the sheriff myself, and who knows what I might let accidentally slip out." Before Audra could say a word, a guard came over and bent to speak to Lexine. Without sparing another glance at Audra she hung up, shoved back her chair and followed the guard from the room.

As Audra watched them leave, a sick feeling invaded her stomach. She'd better pray the sheriff arrested that waitress soon, before Lexine decided that Audra herself was expendable.

Brandon could tell that the sheriff's phone call had upset Emma, but she insisted she was fine. He'd brought her back out to the ranch after breakfast, intending to give her a riding lesson if she was willing. Instead they'd run into Garrett, Collin, and Rand Harding, the ranch manager, all seated around the kitchen table having a discussion when Brandon and Emma had walked in.

He could tell Emma was nervous when he introduced her, but Garrett and the others quickly made
her welcome. She must have recognized his grandfather and half brother from the Black Boot, but she
didn't let on. Rand remembered her from when he'd
taken his wife and baby to the café for lunch. Emma
had heated a bottle for them.

Brandon was afraid they'd interrupted a private discussion, but Garrett insisted they help themselves to
coffee and join the three of them at the table.

"We're talking strategy," he explained to both
Brandon and Emma. "That damn Jordan Baxter's
been bragging about blocking our purchase of the
ranch, and we're trying to figure out what to do
next." He tipped his head at Emma. "Begging your
pardon, but the Baxters have been a thorn in our sides
for a good long while."

"That's putting it mildly," Brandon interjected,
"considering that one of them murdered your uncle
and your cousin."

The talk of violence must have upset Emma, who
seemed to stiffen. "Who was that?" she asked.

"A witch named Lexine," Garrett replied. "She's
up at the women's prison." He shook his head. "A
life sentence is better than she deserves. Woman or
not, they should have strung her up."

Angrily, Garrett banged his fist on the table. "Jordan Baxter isn't going to win this one," he exclaimed. "We'll get around him and someday this
ranch will be your legacy, yours and your brothers'."

Brandon had tried before to explain that he'd done

quite well for himself back in Nevada and didn't need the ranch, but Garrett had refused to listen. Brandon had even thought about offering to help financially with the legal battle, but now wasn't the time.

"How do you like Whitehorn?" Garrett asked Emma, abruptly changing the subject.

If she was startled by the direct question, she recovered quickly. "It's a nice town," she replied. "I've met some friendly people here."

Garrett asked her a few more questions about herself, things Brandon already knew. He was about to make an excuse and extricate Emma when she mentioned something that surprised him.

"I'd like to make use of my teaching degree someday," she said shyly in response to Garrett's query about her job at the Hip Hop. "If I stay around, I might look into getting accredited here in Montana."

"I didn't know you taught," Brandon blurted.

She glanced down at her hands. "Only my student teaching. After I graduated, there weren't any openings back home, so I got a job in an insurance office."

"And what brings you to our state?" Garrett asked.

"Now, Granddad, her reasons may be personal," Collin chided gently. He smiled at Emma. "Don't mind us. All we normally have to talk to is cows and each other. We get a little nosy when a real person comes around and then we forget what little manners we've got." Collin glanced at Brandon. "Ain't that right, bro?"

"Speak for yourself," Brandon drawled. "My

manners are just fine.'' He winked at Emma to let her know she was off the hook. "Aren't they?"

"You have lovely manners,'' she assured him. "Now if I could just get you to use a fork and spoon..." Deliberately she let the sentence trail off as she shook her head sadly.

Rand leaned forward and slapped the table with his hand. "We noticed that, too,'' he said as Garrett guffawed at Emma's teasing. "First time I've ever seen a slob use a finger bowl.''

"And extend his pinkie when he drinks tea,'' Collin added with a mocking gesture.

"Yeah, yeah.'' Brandon got to his feet. "If you're going to tell family secrets, we're out of here.'' He looked down at Emma, relieved to see she was grinning. "Come on, honey, and I'll show you the horses. They're a lot more interesting that these jackasses.''

"Come back anytime,'' Garrett told her as she said her goodbyes. "In fact, why don't you stay for dinner? We eat at five.''

Emma glanced at Brandon, who had other ideas for how they'd be spending their evening. "Okay if we take a rain check?'' he asked.

"Sure thing, as long as you promise to bring her back real soon.''

"I'll look forward to it,'' Emma said. Some of the strain Brandon had seen in her expression earlier when his grandfather had been ranting about the Baxters was back again. All that talk about murder must have reminded her of the business with the sheriff. She was probably more worried about it than she was willing to let on. Maybe Brandon could distract her once he got her away from the house and they found a little privacy. The least he could do was try.

Seven

"No one will bother us here. Make love with me, Emma."

Brandon had been showing her around the barn and the stables. Since they'd left the main house, they hadn't run into another soul. The building they were in now was used to store a jumble of haying equipment that wouldn't be utilized again until the end of the summer. It was quiet and cool here, the only light coming from several high windows. The faint smells of dried grass and diesel weren't unpleasant. Rather, they added to the feeling of tranquillity.

Off in an alcove, by itself, was a cot covered with a plaid blanket.

Since the beginning of their tour, Brandon had been stealing kisses at every opportunity, each one longer and more intense, until it was all Emma could do to pay any attention to the animals and equipment he'd been pointing out for the past half hour.

Now he watched her with a hooded expression, waiting for her answer. After Garrett's comments about the destruction Lexine had wrought in the Kincaid family, Emma felt like the worst kind of fraud for setting foot on their land. Perhaps she had no right to be here, but she couldn't walk away from Brandon as long as he professed to need her.

"Emma?" he asked. "No one will bother us here, I promise." Desire darkened his eyes and pulled the skin taut across his cheekbones—the same desire that bubbled through her veins like champagne. How could she deny him what they both wanted? How could she tell him about her lineage and watch the heat in his gaze turn cold with disdain?

With a hungry sigh she melted into his arms and lifted her face for his kiss. Tonight he would leave her again, but for now he was hers and she wasn't going to waste one precious minute regretting things she couldn't change.

The narrow cot hadn't stopped Brandon from claiming her with a raw urgency that still brought a smile to Emma's lips the next morning. She didn't have to be at the Hip Hop for a couple of hours yet, but she wanted time to look through her cookbook for some recipes to prepare when Brandon came back. He wasn't even gone from her twelve hours and she missed him already.

She was sitting at the table nursing a cup of coffee and flipping through the section on casseroles when someone knocked at the door. Her first thought was that Brandon had come back, but she knew he'd left this morning for Reno. He'd already postponed that meeting once for her sake. Perhaps it was Janie at the door. Although she was careful not to encroach on

Emma's privacy, she did drop by occasionally for a cup of coffee and a visit.

Emma pulled open the door with a smile on her face that froze when she recognized the uniformed officer standing in front of her.

Sheriff Rawlings.

"I'm sorry to bother you," he said, removing his gray Stetson and smoothing his hand through his hair, "but I have a few more questions."

She would have liked to shut the door in his face, but she knew he was only doing his job. It happened to be her tough luck that she'd been drawn into his investigation, but that didn't mean it would be prudent to alienate him, especially when her own landlord was one of his deputies. Eventually Emma would be cleared and she could put this episode behind her.

"Come on in." She stood back and held the door open wider. Then she had a sudden thought. "Are you here with the results from the DNA test?" she asked hopefully.

He walked into the room before he turned to face her. "You sound eager to hear back on that."

"Of course I am. That test will prove I've been telling the truth. So you haven't heard?" she asked, disappointed.

"Not yet, but I've got a friend at the lab who promised to do what he could to speed things up." He raised a warning hand. "It could still take a couple of weeks, but that's not why I'm here."

"Would you like some coffee?" Emma asked. It wouldn't hurt to be polite. She'd brewed a pot this morning instead of settling for her usual instant and there was enough left for another cup.

The solemn set of his features relaxed. Although he didn't actually smile, he was still attractive in a brooding way. His neatly pressed gray uniform added to his quiet air of authority. The black leather of his holster matched that of his boots. Although he wasn't anyone she would want for an enemy, she'd heard he was scrupulously fair and honest.

"Coffee would be nice." He followed her into the kitchen. While she filled a mug, he hovered, declining her offer of sugar and milk.

"Are you comfortable here?" he asked once they were seated across from each other at the table and he'd set down his hat.

"It's fairly compact, but I like it," she replied, impatient to hear why he'd come. "I don't need a lot of space."

"I helped Reed put in the shower stall," he volunteered, "and I laid the carpet."

Emma couldn't think of a comment, so she nodded and sipped her own lukewarm coffee. A glance at the clock told her she still had plenty of time before she needed to leave for work.

He must have noticed the direction of her gaze. "Am I keeping you from something?"

"No, but you said you had more questions and I'm curious about what else I could possibly tell you."

"Of course you are." He set down his mug and laced his fingers together. They were long, with neatly trimmed nails. A plain gold wedding band gleamed against his dark skin. "I told you I was going to talk to Lexine and I did, but my conversation with her made me curious about something."

"What's that?" What could she have told him about Emma? The two women had only seen each other that one time.

"Before I go into it, would you mind telling me what your relationship with her is like? Do you get along?"

Emma shrugged. "I've only seen her once, and that was a disaster. She's a bitter woman, full of anger, and I guess I disappointed her when I wasn't properly sympathetic to her hard-luck story. Frankly, I was appalled that she blamed her victims for their own murders. She got angry, we quarreled and I left. I haven't decided whether I'll go back or not."

"I'm sorry," he replied, steepling his fingers. "It must have been doubly disappointing after you'd taken the trouble to find her."

"Yes, it was." Emma was still struggling to let go of the loving reunion she'd fantasized about for most of her life. "When I was growing up, she refused to relinquish her rights so that I could be adopted. I always believed that meant she planned to come back for me." Emma paused to swallow the lump that had risen into her throat. Lexine's rejection still hurt. "I wanted to meet her and find out why she left me behind in the first place. I'd convinced myself that she had no choice." Emma realized she was chattering, telling him more than he'd asked. Abruptly she clamped her lips together. Wasn't that how cops tried to trip a person up, to get them talking so they said something they hadn't intended to?

"Who knows why a woman like Lexine acts the way she does." There was genuine anger in the sheriff's voice. In his career he'd probably seen plenty of families who'd been torn apart for one reason or another. "That kind of behavior is something rational people can't figure out, because their brains don't work in the same way as someone like hers does."

His comment sounded personal, as though he was well acquainted with Lexine. Was it possible that some of her crimes had touched his family, just as they had Brandon's? Before Emma could ask, he leaned forward.

"There's something I probably should have told you when you were in my office," he said in a clipped tone. "It's no secret, but neither is it something I go around bragging about."

What could he be trying to say? He looked distinctly uncomfortable, but it couldn't have anything to do with Emma. Before she'd been in his office, she'd only exchanged a few words with him at the café.

"What is it?" she asked warily.

He took a sip of coffee, his knuckles pale against the handle of the mug. When he set it back down, his throat worked as he swallowed. Emma braced herself, not knowing why she was suddenly fearful.

"Lexine's my mother, too," he said flatly. "You're my half sister."

For a moment Emma merely gaped at him, trying

to absorb the meaning of his startling words. She'd heard the bizarre stories that Rafe Rawlings was abandoned in the woods as a baby and raised by wolves, but she'd discounted them and his nickname of "Wolf Boy" as being nothing more than cruel gossip manufactured by his enemies.

The sheriff's smile was crooked. "It's true," he insisted when she continued to stare without speaking. "You and I are related, so maybe you'd better call me Rafe—at least in private."

Finally she shook off the paralysis that had taken hold of her tongue. "How can that be?" she asked.

He sat back in the chair as the wood creaked in protest. He was a big man, solidly built, with a wide chest and muscular arms. His shoulders would have looked broad even without the epaulets on his uniform shirt. For the first time, Emma was curious about him as a person, but she could see no family resemblance between the dark-haired man seated across from her and the face she saw in the mirror each morning.

"Lexine had numerous affairs," he replied, his lip curling with distaste, "most of them with married men. My father was a man named Charles Avery."

"Then why is your name Rawlings?" Emma blurted.

He ducked his head and red tinged his cheekbones. "The Rawlings took me in. They're the only parents I've ever known."

Emma thought of the couple who had eventually rescued her from the foster care system. She wanted to touch his hand, but she didn't quite dare. "Are they still alive?" she asked instead.

"My mother is. She lives near here."

This news was hard for Emma to assimilate, especially when she recalled how she'd agonized over admitting why she'd come to Whitehorn! Someone else besides this staunchly professional man seated across from her might have found her dilemma amusing, confessing her secret parentage to her own half brother. How much better she would have felt if he'd enlightened her right away!

"Why didn't you tell me when I was in your office?" she demanded.

"You know having Lexine Baxter for a birth mother isn't exactly something you want to brag about." His tone was dry. "Besides, you caught me by surprise."

She suspected that wasn't an admission he made often. "So why are you telling me now?" she asked. "Did you figure I'd find out anyway?"

"No, that wasn't why, even though it's common knowledge. I told you I went to see her. Even knowing you two didn't hit it off doesn't explain why she tried to convince me of your guilt."

His words stunned Emma even more than his previous announcement had. Did Lexine hate her, based on one unfortunate meeting? Had she never cared for Emma at all? The idea brought tears to her eyes and she had to look away.

"Are you okay?" Rafe asked roughly.

She took a deep, shuddering breath. It was time she

realized her relationship with her birth mother was never going to be the stuff of fairy tales. "I'm fine." Even to her own ears, her voice had a hollow ring.

"So, do you have any idea why she'd try to make you look suspicious?" Rafe prodded, his tone slightly more gentle.

"What did she say?" Emma asked, mentally bracing herself.

Unsnapping the flap on his shirt pocket, he removed a small notebook and flipped it open, but he barely glanced at whatever he'd written. "She told me that you have a nasty temper and it's her opinion that you might be capable of violence." He was watching Emma carefully, gauging her reaction to what he was telling her, but she wasn't sure if he felt sorry for her or was merely studying her in the same manner as he would any other suspect. "She also said you mentioned that you'd explored the woods on several occasions last summer."

Emma's mouth fell open. "That's a lie," she gasped. "It never came up. Why would she deliberately try to implicate me?"

"That's what I'm wondering," he replied as he put the notebook back into his pocket. "Whenever anyone's too helpful, it makes me a little nervous."

Emma sent him a pleading look. "She's making it all up. Everything I told you before was the truth. I was here with Brandon that night. He left while I was asleep."

Before she could continue with her litany, the sheriff cut in. "I'm beginning to believe you, and it has nothing to do with our relationship. There are just too many holes. The only reason I can think of that Lexine would want to implicate you would be to divert suspicion from someone else."

That idea hadn't occurred to Emma. "But who?" she asked.

"Good question." He slid back his chair and got to his feet. "I'm going to give my contact at the lab another call, and I'll keep you posted. In the meantime, try not to worry." For the first time, he cracked a smile. "Easy to say, right?"

She bobbed her head in agreement, but his words helped to reassure her. "Thank you."

He picked up his hat and headed for the door. With his hand on the knob, he turned back to Emma. "One more thing," he said. "My wife, Raeanne, said to welcome you to the family."

His words made Emma realize she was actually connected to people here in Whitehorn, something that hadn't occurred to her when Rafe had mentioned Lexine.

"Do you have children?" she asked, remembering the photo she'd seen in his office.

His expression softened. "We have a daughter named Skye. She's four." He took a snapshot from his wallet and showed her. It was a smaller version of the other picture.

"You have an attractive family," Emma said as she handed back the photo.

After he'd put it away, he stepped outside and settled his hat back onto his head. "They'd both like to meet you."

Emma was about to suggest they get together when she realized what an awkward position it could put him in. Her smile was wry. "Let's put that off until after we get the DNA results," she said instead.

He frowned and then he patted her shoulder awkwardly. "That's not necessary. Raeanne works in the public defender's office and they're pretty busy right now, but I'll have her call you the first chance she gets. We'll have you over." He hesitated again. "Meanwhile, let me know if you need anything or even if you just want to talk."

Until she was cleared, she could hardly confide in him, but she thanked him, anyway. Other than Lexine, Rafe was the first blood relative Emma had ever met. Despite their adversarial positions, she was eager to get to know him better. "I'll look forward to meeting your wife and your daughter," she added. "Tell them I said hello."

He touched his fingers to the brim of his hat in a casual salute. "Will do. I'll be in touch."

Emma watched him head down the steps. Before he got into his black-and-white Jeep Cherokee with the official insignia on the door, he glanced up and waved. Perhaps she'd gained another ally. With Brandon, that made at least two people who believed in her. One question nagged at Emma. Why wasn't her own mother one of them?

* * *

As soon as Emma reported for work, Janie came hurrying over. "Rand told me the sheriff came by to see you this morning," she said in a low voice. "Don't worry, Rand wasn't spilling any official department secrets. He drove by the house and saw Rafe's Jeep parked next to the garage." She squeezed Emma's arm. "Are you okay?"

"I'm fine," Emma replied in an undertone. "The sheriff was just touching base, but he hasn't gotten back the test results that will prove I wasn't anywhere near those woods."

Janie looked disappointed. She glanced over her shoulder at Melissa North, the owner of the Hip Hop, who was ringing up a customer's check. "She heard you were being questioned," Janie told Emma, dropping her voice even lower. "She hasn't said anything about it."

"Do you think I should talk to her?" Emma asked. What would she do if she lost this job?

"I already did," Janie replied.

"Wow, thanks," Emma said, grateful for her friend's support.

Janie gave her arm a squeeze before letting go. "I also pointed out that the publicity could be good for business. You know how people love a hint of scandal."

Emma experienced a sinking feeling. What if someone dug into her background and found out about her connection to Lexine? She could see the headlines: Murder Runs In The Family. "Maybe no one will know," she said hopefully.

Janie looked doubtful. "This is a small town and word has a way of getting around."

From her spot at the register, Melissa cleared her throat loudly.

"We'd better both get to work," Janie said. "I just wanted to tell you not to worry about your job."

After thanking Janie for her consideration and support, Emma went in the back to stow away her purse. The lunch rush was heavier than usual, so she didn't have much time to think about Rafe or Lexine until her break a couple of hours later. Even then all she wanted to do was to call Brandon and tell him about her new brother, but she couldn't do that without spilling the beans about Lexine.

Emma had no choice but to keep the news to herself, along with Lexine's attempt to cast suspicion on her. The list of things Emma couldn't tell Brandon was growing. She'd have to be careful about what she said around him or she was bound to make a slip.

When Brandon pulled into the café parking lot two days later, every spot was taken. Surprised, he glanced at his Rolex. The breakfast rush was over; at this time of day the Hip Hop should be half empty. Instead he could see people standing in the entry.

He'd called Emma a couple of times while he was gone, but he could sense the growing distance between them as though she was guarding every word she said. He'd asked what was wrong, but she kept insisting she was fine. Finally he'd canceled meetings, cleared his calendar and raced back to Whitehorn. As the miles went by, he told himself it was worry and not the burning hunger to hold her in his arms that drove him. Now that he was about to see her again, that argument turned mighty pale.

After he'd parked in the alley and walked around to the front door, he could see that he'd been right. The place was packed right down to the seats at the counter and there was a line waiting for tables.

As he searched for a glimpse of Emma, Janie spotted him and came hurrying over. "I'm so glad you're here," she said fervently.

"What's going on? Is Emma okay?" he asked, sudden alarm threatening to choke him.

Janie glanced over her shoulder. "There was a column in this morning's newspaper about the investigation."

"They didn't give her name, did they?" Brandon snapped. If they had, he'd bring a lawsuit that would keep them in court for years. Talk about irresponsible reporting!

"Not since she hasn't been charged, but they offered enough details for anyone with an IQ over sixty to figure out her identity and turn this place into a circus." Janie sounded as disgusted as he felt.

"Why didn't you send Emma home?" he demanded as his gaze swept the café and he finally saw her coming from the kitchen carrying a large order. Someone seated at the counter said something to her that she ignored, but her face flamed and her eyes flashed.

"I tried to get her to leave," Janie said, "but she

refused. Charlene and her boyfriend are in Reno and you can see how busy we are. I have to admire Emma's grit, but it's got to be hard for her."

"Perhaps I'd better see if I can get her to leave," he suggested as he saw another customer reach for Emma's arm when she hurried past.

"Good idea," Janie told him. "She's got tomorrow off, so maybe this will all blow over by the next day." She sucked in a breath. "Oh, damn," she muttered as the man who'd failed in getting Emma's attention got to his feet, lurching slightly.

Brandon stiffened. "What's wrong?"

"Those two guys have been troublemakers since high school," Janie said. "Josh Derosier is probably already half drunk and it isn't even noon. He's always picking fights and I know of at least one tavern that's barred him for life. Roy Brant, the guy with him, is just as bad. I'd better get over there before they cause any problems."

Bemused, Brandon watched her confront the two men wearing dirty work clothes. They were both in need of shaves and haircuts. Janie wasn't very big and they towered over her, but she was fearless. Before Brandon could react, the man she'd referred to as Josh pushed her aside and headed toward Emma, who was serving a party seated in one of the booths.

"Hey, murderess," he called, stopping all conversation in the café. "How did it feel to kill that woman?"

Enraged, Brandon dove through the crowd. Emma set down the plates she'd been carrying and turned to

confront Derosier. Her face had gone pale, but her
chin went up and she stood tall.

"I didn't kill anyone," she said firmly, her voice
carrying through the shocked silence like a shout.

The new busboy, who was too busy gawking to
watch where he was going, plowed into Brandon and
dropped the loaded tray he'd been carrying with a
loud crash. Swearing under his breath, Brandon
ducked around the kid and the mess. This scene was
too much like the one with Homer Gilmore.

"That's enough!" Janie told the two men taunting
Emma. "Both of you get out and don't come back."

"But I wanna know how she did it," Roy almost
whined.

Brandon watched as Emma's tortured gaze darted
from the two of them to the other customers who were
watching the grim tableau, but no one stepped forward to defend her. The avid curiosity on their faces
made Brandon sick. These were the same people
she'd been serving for months and now all of a sudden she'd been tried and convicted in their eyes.

Fury roared through Brandon as he joined Emma
in the center of attention. He struggled to control his
temper, well aware of just how easy it would be to
start a melee that could get innocent people hurt and
wreck Emma's place of employment.

He stared down each of the two men. Josh was as
tall as Brandon, but thinner. Roy was shorter, with a
gut that hid his buckle. Beyond their sneering ex-
pressions, they didn't look bright enough to scare up
two brain cells between them.

Brandon swallowed his disgust as Roy elbowed Josh and they both laughed. "How'd the two of you like to step outside?" Brandon suggested. "Or is it only women you deal with?"

Roy started to back away, but Josh took a swing. Luckily it missed Brandon by a foot, although the momentum spun Josh around and nearly knocked him over.

"I called the sheriff's office on my cell phone," someone shouted from the back of the crowd. "They're on their way."

"Be careful," Emma implored from behind Brandon. "Don't get hurt."

"Is this dude your accomplice?" Josh asked as he straightened. He looked at Roy, who was hanging back, and both of them giggled.

"This dude is more than that," Brandon snarled as fresh anger threatened his control. Adrenaline pumping, he grabbed both men by the backs of their shirt collars and hustled them toward the door. Like the Red Sea, the crowd of staring onlookers parted. His intention was to toss them both out the door, but as he reached the front of the café, two sheriff's vehicles pulled up, lights flashing, and the drivers jumped out.

In a moment it was over. One deputy took the men in custody while the other stuck around to take witness statements and fill out his report. Most of the people he talked to agreed that the assault had been unprovoked. The lone man who started to say something about Emma was quickly silenced by a look from Brandon. He'd expected her to be in tears, but she insisted on talking to the deputy herself. By the time they were through, most of the customers had finished their meals and departed. Finally the deputy gave Emma his business card and left.

Brandon circled a protective arm around Emma. "Let's get out of here."

"I'm not through with my shift," she protested with a nervous glance at Melissa.

Before she could duck away, the woman she'd referred to came up to them. "Thanks for coming to our aid," she said after Emma had introduced Brandon to her. "Getting those boys out of here was quick thinking on your part. Why don't you come back sometime for a steak dinner on the house?"

Surprised, Brandon thanked her. He was about to ask if Emma could take the rest of the day off, but before he could say anything, Melissa took her hand and patted it. "I think you should stay home for a few days, until this blows over."

For the first time since the ugly incident had started, Brandon saw tears fill Emma's eyes. He tightened his arm around her protectively. "Why are you punishing her? She hasn't done anything wrong."

"I know that," Melissa said. "Believe me, if I was thinking of my bottom line, I'd work her double shifts. Did you notice how busy we were? You couldn't have wedged another party in here with a shoe horn. Some women might enjoy being gawked at and whispered about, but I don't think our Emma's one of them." She glanced around the café and then she gave Emma a considering stare.

"You look wrung out," she said bluntly. "Get some rest." She glanced at Brandon. "Don't do a lot of heavy fretting about this. In a couple of days there'll be something new to occupy their tiny minds. Your job will still be here. How's that sound?"

Brandon felt Emma tremble. "I'll come back on Thursday," she offered.

Melissa smiled. "I'll be expecting you," she said. Before either of them could thank her, she hurried away.

He suspected that all the fight had drained out of Emma. "Come on," he urged. "Let's go by your place and pick up a few clothes."

"What for?" she asked with a bewildered expression.

He gave her a reassuring grin. "I'm taking you back to the city that never sleeps. Reno, here we come!"

Eight

Despite the strain of the past hour, Emma felt a surge of excitement at Brandon's offer to take her to Nevada with him. How wonderful it would be to leave her troubles here in Whitehorn and spend a couple of days with the man who had become so important to her.

"What do you think?" he asked as they crossed the café parking lot. "We can laze by the pool, hit some casinos if you want, catch a show. I'll take you shopping. We'll check out the sights." His expression softened. "Come with me," he coaxed. "Like Melissa said, in a couple of days this will have all blown over. Maybe the sheriff will hear back on the blood test by then, too."

The blood test! The *investigation*. Emma's excitement deflated like a balloon with a leak.

"He told me not to leave town," she wailed. "I'm stuck right here in Whitehorn."

Brandon's smile faded, and then he snapped his fingers. "We'll talk to him. I'm sure that as long as he knows where we're going and when we'll be back, he can make an exception. Come on, we can swing by his office on the way." Brandon began walking more quickly, pulling her along with him.

Emma stopped in her tracks, the movement freeing her hand from his loose clasp. "I can't ask him for any favors," she said flatly. Even if Rafe was willing to let her go, she couldn't presume on their very new relationship by asking for special treatment.

Brandon whipped around to stare at her. "Why the hell not?" he demanded. "You have to be back by Thursday for work and we both know these charges are bogus."

Grateful for his wholehearted endorsement of her innocence, Emma still had to come up with a plausible reason to not bother Rafe. "I don't think I could enjoy myself with this hanging over me," she said lamely.

Brandon was instantly contrite. "Of course you can't. I'm sorry, sweetie. How arrogant of me to figure being with me would magically make it all disappear." He traced his finger down her cheek. "I just wanted to distract you for a little while."

Oh, great. Now he didn't think he was capable of claiming a hundred percent of her attention. She wanted to tell him that when he kissed her, she forgot about everything else, but circumstances didn't permit that kind of candor.

"It was a nice idea, though," she offered, barely able to meet his gaze. How she would have loved for him to show her his city, the house where he lived, and maybe his office building, too. "Could I have a rain check?"

He lifted her hand and pressed his lips to her knuckles. "Of course. But I have another idea, one that won't get you in trouble with the local gendarmes.''

''What's that?'' she asked despondently.

''Come and stay at the ranch for a few days. We have plenty of spare bedrooms if you feel uncomfortable about bunking with me while you're there. I'll teach you to ride. What do you think?'' He was grinning again, his enthusiasm restored.

How could Emma bear being around the Kincaids, knowing the pain Lexine had caused them by murdering Jeremiah and Dugin? Emma was too afraid some hint of her own dirty secret would show on her face like a scarlet letter.

Sadly she shook her head, twisting the truth again. ''I'd rather just go home.''

Brandon's smile faded and a closed look came over his face. ''Okay, if that's what you want,'' he said briskly. ''Just let me follow you to make sure you get there safely.''

She knew her refusal had hurt him. He was taking it as a personal rejection. Would they never get the situation right between them?

''I'm sorry,'' she said softly.

He avoided her beseeching gaze. ''If you'll just wait for me here, I'll bring my car around.'' He didn't say anything more about spending time together, and the next two days without work to keep Emma busy stretched out in front of her like a jail sentence.

Poor choice of words! The unfortunate comparison made her shiver as she watched him walk quickly away, his shoulders rigid and his hands bunched at his sides.

Once Emma got to her apartment, she saw that a news van was blocking the driveway and two unfamiliar cars were pulled up to the curb. By the time she'd stopped behind the van and Brandon had parked his Lexus, four people had rushed up to her car. As Emma got out, she could hear a camera shutter going off.

"Did you do it?" someone shouted. Another voice called her by name and a man with a video camera hurried over. "Why'd you kill her?" a young woman asked, shoving a microphone in Emma's face. "Did you know the victim? Was the father of her baby your lover?"

The ferocity of the shouted questions stunned Emma as she pressed against the side of her car. The cameraman blocked the staircase. She couldn't seem to move. Part of her regretted Brandon seeing this; another part sought him out as the small group crowded closer, their questions increasing in both volume and frequency.

"Have you gotten an attorney?"

"Is this your new lover?"

"Were you jealous of Christina?"

Once again Brandon came to her aid, frowning darkly as he took her elbow in a firm grip.

"I've already called the sheriff and he's on his way," he announced as he shoved aside the microphone and glared at the reporter. "This is private property. You're all trespassing. If you don't leave, I promise you we'll press charges.''

Immediately the video camera swung toward him. ''What's your name?'' demanded the woman. ''Were you with Emma that night?''

Brandon never glanced at her. Instead he hustled Emma up the stairs to her apartment as she dug frantically in her bag for her key. Her hands were shaking so badly that she nearly dropped it. When she struggled with the lock, footsteps pounded up the stairs behind them and the chorus of questions grew louder. Brandon shoved her inside and slammed the door shut behind them. He flipped the lock and Emma fell against the closed panel, panting like an out-of-shape cocker spaniel. When someone rattled the knob, she leaped away with a muffled shriek, and then the doorbell started ringing.

Moaning, Emma pressed her hands to her ears until it stopped. ''How did they find out my address?'' she exclaimed softly after she'd caught her breath. ''I'm unlisted.'' As if on cue, the telephone rang.

Brandon looked out the window. ''Don't answer that! It looks like that witch with the mike is calling you on her cell phone.''

Emma snatched back her hand. A siren sounded in the distance and she sent up a silent thank-you to Rafe for acting so quickly.

''With computers, we have no secrets left,'' Brandon replied as she joined him at the window. ''If they want to, they can find out everything about you, right down to your bra size.''

Everything? Even a person's lineage? A chill went through Emma as the siren grew louder. Suddenly the group below began scrambling for their vehicles. In a flash, the cars and van were gone.

"Thank heavens," Emma muttered with a sigh of relief, turning away from the window.

"They'll be back," Brandon predicted. "Or more like them. It looks like you're getting your fifteen minutes of fame."

With a sick heart, she realized she couldn't stay here, not with cars and reporters hounding her and disturbing the neighbors. "Is the offer to go to the ranch still open?" she asked timidly.

If the reason for her change of heart hurt his feelings, he didn't let it show. "Sure thing," he said with a crooked grin as more footsteps sounded on the stairs outside.

"Oh, no," she groaned, her defenses depleted.

"Relax, it's the sheriff." Brandon flipped the lock and opened the door to admit Rafe Rawlings.

"Are you okay?" he demanded when he saw Emma. Did Brandon notice the extent of his concern?

Emma folded her arms across her chest. "I'm fine now. I was just caught unprepared."

Briefly, Brandon described the scene to the sheriff.

He shook his head. "Is there someone else you can stay with for a few days? A friend?"

"That's what I've been trying to get her to do," Brandon replied.

Here was Emma's chance to ask about Reno, but she was afraid if Rafe agreed, Brandon might start to wonder just why he'd made an exception for the prime suspect in an active murder investigation. "I'm going with Brandon to his family's ranch," she said quickly.

"Good idea," Rafe replied. He glanced at Brandon. "Just be careful you aren't followed. Even if one of those jackals runs your plates, it won't clue them to the ranch." He looked back at Emma and his gaze softened imperceptibly. "They'll lose interest as soon as another story comes along," he predicted.

"I hope so," she said fervently. "It was awful, like sharks on a feeding frenzy."

"Throw a few clothes in a bag," Brandon said. "We'll get going before they come back."

It didn't take Emma long to pack. They decided to leave her car at the apartment as a decoy, and the sheriff suggested she close the curtains, as well.

By the time she and Brandon finally drove through the gates to the ranch, minus any signs of a tail, she was exhausted. At least she felt as if she'd put the incident in perspective.

"How are you doing?" Brandon asked. He'd been silent for the last couple of miles, but he'd kept her hand clasped in his after calling ahead to let Garrett know they were coming.

"Better than I was," Emma replied, covering a yawn with her free hand. "I wonder how celebrities cope with the press when they face it all the time."

"I'm sure it gets old." He squeezed her hand. "I thought you did very well."

His comment warmed her. She wanted his approval, and she had worried that all this negative attention she'd been getting might affect his feelings toward her, whatever they might be.

As soon as he pulled the car up behind the main house, Garrett and Collin came out to meet them. Garrett opened Emma's door as Brandon grabbed her bag from behind the seat.

"I'm sorry about what happened back at your place," Garrett said after Brandon filled him in. "I'm glad Brandon brought you here. If anyone dares to set foot on our property, we'll give them a real cowboy welcome." The chill in his eyes belied his words and made Emma glad she wasn't his enemy. Would he feel the same—would any of them—when the truth about Lexine came out?

"We'll take good care of you," Collin added with a smile.

Emma was warmed by their support. "Thank you," she said, glancing at Brandon. "I'm glad to be here."

"The housekeeper left us, but Cookie sent up a pot of beef stew and homemade biscuits from the bunkhouse," Garrett volunteered. "There's apple pie and ice cream for dessert."

His words brought an answering growl from Emma's stomach that was loud enough to make all four of them chuckle as they trooped up the back steps to the kitchen. The savory aromas of good food welcomed them inside.

"Is there something I can do to get supper on?" Emma asked, glancing around the immaculate kitchen. Although it was old-fashioned, with dark wood and dated appliances, the room was big and homey. She wanted to make it clear from the start that she didn't expect to be waited on, especially after they'd worked hard all day.

Before Garrett could refuse her offer, Brandon cut in. "That's a good idea. I'll help you."

His offer both surprised and pleased Emma, who'd assumed he was accustomed to full-time kitchen help of his own. Every time she tried to put him in a certain compartment, he managed to surprise her.

"Suit yourselves," Garrett said with a shrug. "I still need to wash up. There's salad fixings in the refrigerator, if you feel up to throwing one together." He pointed at the cupboard. "Dishes in there. Silverware in the drawer. We'll just be four tonight, so you can dish up whenever you like."

Emma's stomach growled again.

"Better make it soon," Brandon said dryly.

After Garrett and Collin filed out, Emma took a quick survey. The stew pot was in the oven, the biscuits in a covered basket waiting to be warmed in the microwave sitting on the counter. The black appliance looked like a recent addition.

While Brandon made himself busy setting the table and making coffee, she put together a salad of torn greens, cherry tomatoes and grated carrot. They worked in companionable silence until she opened the oven door, mitts on both hands, and reached for the cast-iron pot.

"Let me do that." In a blink Brandon was beside her.

Emma debated taking a stand, but the pot looked huge and it was probably heavy. "Thank you," she said, handing him the mitts.

While he uncovered the stew, releasing a wonderful aroma, and set the pot on a metal trivet in the middle of the table, she heated the biscuits. She was about to ask him to summon the other men when she heard bootsteps on the hardwood floor. As soon as Garrett and Collin appeared with their damp hair slicked back and wearing clean shirts, Brandon pulled out a chair for Emma.

Once they were all seated, the biscuits and salad were passed. Like the performers in a well-orchestrated dance, Garrett ladled out portions of stew and Collin poured the coffee. For the first few minutes everyone ate silently.

Emma found the stew to be the best she'd ever had and the biscuits feather-light. She looked forward to meeting Cookie and she wondered how Brandon liked the plain, hearty fare. He'd never struck her as a picky eater and he was doing justice to this meal.

She hadn't eaten since breakfast and her appetite was healthy despite the day's traumas. "My compliments to the cook," she said when she'd taken the edge off her hunger.

"I'll pass it along." Garrett set down his spoon and put aside his empty bowl. "Brandon told us a little about the investigation," he said as Emma tensed, a piece of biscuit halfway to her mouth. Perhaps he didn't really want her here. "How are you holding up?"

His warm gaze and gentle voice were nearly her undoing. She swallowed hard and set down the bite of biscuit. Kindness from the very people her mother had hurt so badly was almost more than she could bear.

"I'm okay," she replied with a glance at Brandon. "It's nice of you to put me up, though. I wasn't looking forward to seeing camera lenses sticking in my windows."

"This is Brandon's home and his friends are welcome," Garrett replied.

Emma wondered if that was how Brandon had described their relationship. Then his hand squeezed her knee under the table, as if he could read her thoughts. He didn't say anything, though. Well, what did she want, for him to announce they were lovers?

"Let us know if there's anything we can do," Garrett added. "If anyone else bothers you, they'll have the Kincaids to deal with."

"That's right," Collin added quietly.

Their generosity brought another lump of emotion to Emma's throat and her smile was shaky. "Thank you," she murmured.

As if he sensed her struggle for composure, Brandon changed the subject. "I want to give Emma a riding lesson in the morning," he told Collin. "Which horse would be a good mount for her?"

Collin winked at Emma before he replied. "The same old nag you learned on, bro. It's only been a few months since you lost your greenhorn status, you know.''

While the two men bantered, Emma concentrated on her dinner. Once everyone was done, she served the apple pie and ice cream while Brandon poured more coffee and Collin cleared off the dirty dishes.

''You don't have to do the KP,'' Garrett exclaimed when they were finished and Emma began loading the dishwasher. ''This isn't the Hip Hop.''

''If you don't mind, I'd like to keep busy. Why don't you tell me your schedule? I could take care of the meals while I'm here. The cook must have his hands full feeding the crew.'' She hoped she wasn't being presumptuous, but she'd go crazy if she had too much idle time.

Garrett and Collin exchanged glances.

''I'll help,'' Brandon offered.

''Cookie packs the lunches and sends over our supper, but you could serve it up like tonight and fix breakfast,'' Garrett suggested. ''If you're really sure you don't mind.''

''That's settled, then,'' Emma said briskly as she covered the leftover pie. ''Let me find my way around the kitchen tonight while you men go have your brandy and cigars, or whatever it is you do after the meal.''

''It's usually paperwork or the television,'' Garrett corrected her. He slid back his chair. ''Gentlemen, I think we've been given our marching orders and I suggest we make our escape before she hands us all towels and aprons.''

"I don't mind helping," Brandon said quietly after the other two men had thanked Emma again and left the kitchen. "Are you sure you want to tackle this alone?"

"Do you mind?" she asked. "I could use a few minutes to myself."

He tucked one finger under her chin and lowered his head. "If you insist," he murmured, "but don't stay out here too long."

Emma's mind went blank as his mouth settled on hers, any reply she might have made swallowed up by the rush of sensation she felt when he took her in his arms and deepened the kiss.

"Oops!" exclaimed Collin from the doorway.

Brandon lifted his head with a frown of annoyance, but he kept an arm around Emma to prevent her from pulling away in embarrassment.

Collin was already backing out of the kitchen. "I wanted a toothpick, but it can wait."

Brandon muttered an unflattering comment about jackasses and bad timing that made Emma giggle.

"What was that?" Collin demanded.

"Get your damn toothpick." Brandon's tone was definitely surly as he let Emma go and turned away, jamming his hands into his back pockets.

Collin crossed to the cupboard and found what he wanted. "If he gets out of line," he told Emma after he'd stuck a toothpick into the corner of his mouth, "you just holler."

Brandon snorted with disgust as Emma giggled again. "I'll remember that."

"On second thought, I'd better take him with me," Collin decided. "Come on, Brandon. Cinderella has chores to do." He folded his arms across his chest and propped his hip against the counter as he waited, a twinkle in his eyes.

Reluctantly Brandon followed Collin from the kitchen, grumbling under his breath. When the two men were gone, Emma breathed a sigh of relief and got to work. Sometimes a simple task and a basic routine were the best way to relax.

Brandon sat in a corner of the living room and scrolled through his e-mail on his laptop computer. Several messages needed replies, but he ignored them. It wasn't the movie playing on the big screen TV that kept him from concentrating, though; it was knowing that Emma was nearby.

Sweet, sometimes shy Emma, with eyes that changed from calm gray to mysterious green and made him wonder what she was thinking. Emma, with a smile that warmed him and a laugh that invited him to share the joke. Emma he hated leaving, and that scared him, because she still didn't trust him not to hurt her and he didn't trust himself not to fall for her.

And that was the scariest part of all. Despite what he'd told her, there was no way he intended for either of them to sleep alone while she stayed at the ranch.

His bedroom was in the opposite wing from either his grandfather's or Collin's. The room next to Brandon's was used by another one of his bastard half-brothers when he was in residence, but just happened to be empty this week. Leanne and Cade were still visiting Daisy and Ryder in Texas.

What was it about Emma that enabled her to sneak through Brandon's defenses as no other woman had? Was it the innocent yet honest passion he was able to ignite in her, or the admiration he could see in her eyes whenever he came to her defense? He wasn't used to being anyone's hero.

Hell, he'd worked hard for everything he had and, until recently, it had been enough. He had a family now, a connection he was just beginning to appreciate. Sure, once in a while, in the darkest hours of the night, he'd felt a need for something more, something meaningful.

Perhaps it was Emma's refusal to knuckle under to the cloud of suspicion hanging over her that made her special. All he knew was that when he was with her, the world and its pressures seemed to recede for a while. Just thinking about laying her down on the big bed in his room tonight had him squirming with discomfort.

The other two men were nursing bottles of beer while they watched the movie, which seemed to be nothing more than a string of explosions interspersed with brief exchanges of shouted dialogue. Brandon would much rather think about Emma, even if doing so made the fit of his jeans damned uncomfortable.

He was just about to get up and seek her out when she appeared in the doorway. Her hair had worked loose of its pins and was curling softly around her neck, and her eyes were smudged with fatigue. One look at her and Brandon felt guilty for leaving her in the kitchen alone.

"Hey, Emma," Collin said, hitting the pause button on the remote control, "grab a beer and join us. This movie's nearly over, but the finale should be great. I think they're going to blow up the world as we know it."

"Thanks, but it's been a long day," she replied, her gaze seeking Brandon out as her soft voice stroked his jangling nerves. Even if all they did tonight was fall asleep in each other's arms, it would be enough.

Well, not enough, but he'd survive.

"I think I'll turn in," she said to Brandon. "Um, where have you put my bag?"

"I'll show you." His voice sounded strained to his ears. If the others got wind of his sudden attack of nerves, they'd tease him no end when Emma wasn't around.

Garrett must have seen her fatigue. "Don't worry about messing with breakfast in the morning," he told her. "We'll eat at the bunkhouse so you can sleep in."

"Good idea," Brandon replied as he turned off the computer and got to his feet. "We'll see you two at lunch."

Emma's cheeks turned a pretty shade of pink as he crossed the room to where she was standing and hooked his arm around her. Maybe he didn't have to stake his claim in front of his grandfather and Collin, but he found that he liked the idea. When it came to

Emma, he was getting way too possessive. It was something he'd have to think about when he had more time—but not tonight.

"We'll be turning in, too, as soon as this movie's done," Garrett said. "I'm riding out with Rand tomorrow to check out the calves in the northwest section, so it might be a long day." He stroked his chin. "I doubt we'll see you at noon."

"I'm going into town in the morning," Collin said. "The replacement motor for that water pump finally came in."

With a last impatient nod, Brandon hustled Emma down the hall. When they got to his door, he struggled briefly with his rising desire and then he kissed her cheek.

"The room next to mine is empty, if you want it," he offered.

Emma blinked and looked away. "That's fine."

From the wistful thread in her voice, he realized she'd taken his offer all wrong. Tucking a finger under her chin, he tipped up her head and looked into her eyes. "I'm trying to be a gentleman here," he said dryly. "But it's not what I want."

Some of the pertness returned to her voice. "And what is it that you want?"

Brandon let his actions speak for him. Later, when Emma was sound asleep with her head pillowed on his shoulder and her hair tickling his chin, Brandon still didn't have an answer for that last question she'd fired at him.

When it came to Emma, just what was it he wanted?

Even though Brandon intended to let her sleep in the next morning, it was still early when she appeared in the kitchen wearing jeans and a long-sleeved shirt.

"Good morning," she said softly as if she was reluctant to disturb him.

He'd been seated at the kitchen table with a cup of coffee and the newspaper. The other men had left a couple of hours ago and he'd already made several business calls.

As he returned her greeting, he got to his feet and pulled her into his arms. "How did you sleep?" he asked. Several times in the night the urgent hunger for her that he couldn't assuage had brought him awake, but he'd been reluctant to disturb her. He'd never thought he'd be taking a cold shower with a woman in his bed, but that was exactly what he'd done this morning.

"I slept well," she replied. "How about you?"

The lie danced on his tongue, but refused to be spoken out loud. "I don't need a lot of sleep."

She linked her arms around his neck, her eyes twinkling playfully. "Does that mean a nap later is out of the question?"

His body's instantaneous response to her teasing suggestion left him light-headed. "Why wait?" he demanded, calling her bluff.

"I thought I was getting a riding lesson this morning."

He leaned closer, her scent flooding his brain. "That can be arranged," he whispered directly into her ear. Before she could say anything else, he captured her mouth with his. When he finally released her, the only thought in his head was getting her back to his bedroom. He was about to scoop her into his arms when he heard a car door slam outside.

Who'd be coming by at this hour of the morning and expect to find anyone at the house? Releasing Emma, Brandon crossed to the front window and flipped back the corner of the curtain.

"Is someone here?" she asked.

Brandon's stomach did a slow roll. He didn't like what he was seeing, not one bit. He hadn't realized she was looking over his shoulder until she spoke.

"It's the sheriff," she exclaimed with a sudden lilt to her voice. "Maybe he's gotten the results of the blood test."

Before Brandon could say anything, she'd opened the door and rushed outside. He was following so close that he nearly ran her over when she slammed on the brakes, and he knew she saw what he'd noticed through the window.

The sheriff hadn't come alone, and his expression was much too grim for him to be bringing good news. When his gaze met Emma's, Brandon could have sworn he saw a flash of pain cross the other man's face beneath the brim of his Stetson before he turned expressionless.

The deputy, the same one who'd come to the café,

fell in behind his boss as they both approached the house.

"Good morning, Emma, Brandon," the sheriff said in a flat voice. "May we come in?"

Emma had backed up until she was leaning against Brandon, and he could feel the tremors of alarm shivering through her. Since there was no way any test could match Emma's blood to the crime scene, he couldn't figure out why the sheriff looked so serious, unless he was trying to scare her into admitting something.

The idea made Brandon angry. He tucked her behind him and folded his arms, spotting Collin's pickup coming up the long driveway with a dust plume behind it.

"What is it you want?" Brandon demanded of the sheriff. He felt Emma's light touch on his forearm, but he maintained his defiant stance. If the sheriff was here to harass her in any way, he'd have to go through Brandon first.

"Don't make this any harder than it already is," Sheriff Rawlings said as the deputy shifted to stand at his side.

It must have been clear to the sheriff that they weren't going to be invited inside. He squared his shoulders, his expression grim.

"Emma, we got the results back an hour ago. I'm sorry, but the DNA test we took from you was a match to the blood and tissue samples found at the scene."

Shock slammed into Brandon. From behind him Emma moaned softly.

Had he been wrong about her? After he left her apartment that night, had she gone to the woods and somehow been involved in that poor woman's murder? As soon as the thought formed in his head, he dismissed it as ridiculous. There had to be some other explanation.

"No!" she exclaimed. "That's not possible! I wasn't there." She grabbed Brandon's shirt. "You believe me, don't you? The people at the lab are human. Someone made a mistake."

"They must have mixed up the samples." Brandon's mind raced ahead to what must be done next.

"They're very careful. They ran the test twice." The sheriff put his foot on the bottom step and stared hard at Emma. A muscle jumped in his jaw. "Emma Stover, based on the results of the DNA test and the testimony of an eyewitness, I'm here to arrest you for the murder of Christina Montgomery. You'll have to come with us."

Nine

Emma's worst nightmare had begun.

The familiar list of warnings Rafe recited as he read Emma her Miranda rights barely registered; neither did the snap of the handcuffs on her wrists.

"It's procedure," he said gruffly.

She was dimly aware of Brandon watching her, his face flushed with impotent rage and his hands knotted into fists at his sides as Collin held on to his arm.

When Rafe stood back, Brandon put his arms around her and buried his face in her hair. After he let her go, she saw his lips move, but whatever he said was blocked out by the white noise roaring in her head. Someone put a jacket around her shoulders, but it didn't stop her shivering.

Instead of taking her in his Cherokee as she'd hoped, Rafe helped the deputy put Emma in the back of the other patrol car. As they headed down the driveway, she twisted around to look through the rear window at Brandon. He grew smaller and smaller as he stood watching her departure. She wanted to wave, but the cuffs made that impossible.

A tear rolled down her cheek as she turned back around.

"What's going to happen to me now?" she asked the deputy.

"You'll be booked and arraigned," he replied, glancing in the rearview mirror. "If the judge sets bail and you can pay it, you could be out again by this afternoon."

"What do you mean 'if'?" Emma asked. "Are you saying he might not?"

He shrugged as he slowed and turned onto the main road. "It's a capital crime," was all he said.

Nausea threatened when Emma realized it didn't matter whether or not the judge set bail for her. She didn't have the money to pay it, nor could she afford an attorney. How much would an overworked attorney assigned by the court care that she was innocent?

"I need to talk to someone from the public defender's office right away," she said anxiously. "Can you call them on your radio so they can meet us when we get there?"

"Nope."

"Why not?" Hysteria edged Emma's voice. With the confinement of the handcuffs and the grillwork in front of her, she felt as though she were already in jail.

This time the deputy didn't bother to look in the mirror. "No more questions," he said instead as he accelerated. "Just be quiet until we get to town."

Well, who could blame him, Emma thought cynically. From the deputy's point of view, he had a dangerous criminal in his back seat. This was Whitehorn,

Montana. Regardless of his training, transporting a murderer had to make him just a little nervous.

Emma wished she could remember what Brandon had told her, but she hadn't been able to hear past the buzzing in her ears. Even though he'd hugged her so hard that Collin had to peel him away, she wasn't even sure he still believed in her innocence—not when there was such irrefutable proof she was guilty.

Sick at heart and scared to death, Emma hung her head and closed her eyes in a futile attempt to staunch the flow of tears.

As soon as the squad car transporting Emma had disappeared down the road with the sheriff's Jeep in close pursuit, Brandon turned helplessly to Collin. The indecision gripping Brandon was so unusual that he barely knew how to combat it. He was used to action, to taking charge, but now he wasn't sure what to do first.

"Damn it, I don't even know any attorneys in this state," he growled with frustration. Even though Emma hadn't wanted a lawyer earlier, he should have lined one up, anyway. How could he have allowed himself to be caught so unprepared? He'd just been so sure the DNA test would clear her. None of this made any sense.

"I'll take the Jeep out and get Garrett," Collin offered. "I've got a pretty good idea where they are, and he'll know what to do about finding the best criminal attorney around. Let me take your cell phone so he can make some calls while I drive him back in."

Brandon gave Collin a grateful look and handed him the phone. "I'll use the one in the house to line up the money for bail," he said, thinking ahead. "I've got to change clothes and then I'm going to town to be there for Emma." He ran a hand through his hair, his mind spinning. This was all so unreal. A few minutes ago they'd been looking forward to spending the day together and now she was on her way to jail.

"How will you keep me posted if I don't have my phone?"

"We'll meet you in Whitehorn as soon as we can get there," Collin reassured him. "I'll keep the phone on so you can call us."

"I don't know how this happened," Brandon mumbled half to himself.

"Have you considered that she might be lying?" Collin asked bluntly.

"No, I haven't." He felt guilty as hell for that one second he'd allowed a doubt to creep into his head before he'd banished it, but he wasn't about to admit that to Collin or anyone else. "I know Emma. She's telling the truth."

"Okay, then," Collin said with a nod. He slapped a hand on Brandon's shoulder. "I'd better get moving."

"Thanks," Brandon said absently and then he hurried into the house.

Later in the day, as the time of Emma's arraignment crept closer, Brandon wore a restless path in front of the courthouse while he waited for his grandfather. At least the reporters hanging around the front steps weren't same ones who had been at Emma's apartment. None of them paid the slightest attention to Brandon.

Finally he spotted Collin, Garrett, and an older woman walking from the parking lot. Both men had changed to clean dark jeans and shirts topped by Western-cut jackets. Brandon himself was wearing a suit and tie he'd left at the house on another occasion and had been damned glad to find in his closet.

At the sight of his relatives, the ball of fire burning a hole in his gut abated just a little. When they'd spoken on the phone, Garrett had assured him that one of the best criminal guns in the state kept an office right in Whitehorn. Then he offered to throw his hat in with Brandon's at the arraignment. The Kincaid name was well known in these parts and Brandon prayed it might influence the judge into granting bail.

Brandon was still amazed at how quickly the Kincaid men had sprung to his support, dropping everything else to help him. He'd heard about family loyalty, but he'd never experienced it firsthand. As he watched them hurrying toward him, their images blurred and he had to blink a couple of times to clear his vision.

Now Garrett approached with his arms outstretched. He enfolded Brandon in a brief, hard hug before letting him go again. "How you holding up?" he asked. "How's Emma?"

"I'm fine." Brandon shrugged his shoulders in a vain attempt to loosen the knots of tension digging into him. "Emma's okay, I think. They only let me see her for a couple of minutes." He'd wanted so badly to break her out of there that he'd been trembling with the effort it took to not act on an impulse he knew would only make the situation worse. He was a man accustomed to working within the system, but this time his usual iron control was dangerously near the breaking point.

"She keeps insisting she's innocent, but of course no one in there believes her," he said bitterly. "In their eyes, she's already been tried and convicted."

"The DNA test is pretty damning," said the woman with Garrett. Small and trim, her short gray hair streaked with blond, she looked vaguely familiar. Her face had been lined by time, but her voice was vibrant. Her blue suit matched her eyes and the tasteful pearls at her neck appeared to be genuine.

"This is my grandson, Brandon Harper," Garrett said. "Elizabeth Gardener."

Brandon recognized the name. Not only was she well-known, but unlike some successful criminal attorneys she had a reputation for absolute integrity.

"Call me Elizabeth." She shifted her briefcase and extended her hand. Garrett had told Brandon on the phone that she was his first choice, and he'd warned that she'd be expensive.

"Hang the cost," Brandon had replied at the time. Where he was concerned, there was no price tag on Emma's freedom.

"Murder isn't always black and white," Elizabeth said now. "A client doesn't necessarily have to be innocent for me to give her the best defense I can, but I have to believe I can help her.''

"She didn't do it," Brandon said. "I was with her part of the night it happened—''

Elizabeth's eyes narrowed thoughtfully. ''And that's why you believe in her innocence?''

He shook his head. "I know her," he said simply.

"Are you good for her bail?''

"Absolutely." He didn't care what it cost, he refused to let her sit in jail a minute longer than necessary.

"If you need my help, you've got it," Garrett told him.

"Thanks, Granddad." It was the first time Brandon had called him that. Garrett looked both surprised and pleased as he turned his attention back to Elizabeth.

She stared at the ground for a moment, one hand parked on her hip, and then her head snapped up. ''I'll talk to her.''

Brandon knew he had no real reason yet to feel relieved, but this woman inspired a certain degree of confidence. For now that would have to be enough.

"Thank you so much," Emma mumbled against Brandon's chest as he held her tight. For the umpteenth time today she blinked back tears, but at least these were from the sheer relief of being out on bail and not from her earlier despair. How did Lexine get through the day, knowing she would never be free again?

When Brandon released Emma from his embrace,

she took in a deep breath of air and looked up at the sky. She'd never realized before how much in life she took for granted. If she got through this, she vowed silently, she would make some changes.

"And thank *you*," Emma told the attorney Brandon and Garrett had hired on her behalf. "It's good to be free."

Even though they'd ducked out of the courthouse by a side door, two reporters had been waiting for Emma. They'd finally given up after the attorney refused repeatedly to answer their questions or to let Emma say a word. Before the rest of the reporters camped out front had a chance to wise up, Elizabeth had hurried the group to the parking lot, where they now stood.

Emma had seen Elizabeth Gardener on television, but she'd never imagined they'd meet, and certainly not under these circumstances. In person Elizabeth looked much more approachable than she did on TV.

"You're not free. You're merely out on bail," she corrected Emma. "And despite the DNA test, you claim to be innocent."

"It's no claim," Emma retorted. Here was one more person who didn't believe her. "I've never been in those woods."

Elizabeth exchanged glances with Garrett. "Either she's a damn good liar or something else is going on here." She swung her attention back to Emma, who was too strung out by the day's events to summon up much outrage. At least the attorney had left the door open a crack.

"I'm going to follow my instincts," she said with another quick glance at Garrett. "Emma, I know today has been one of the most difficult you've ever faced, but if you're up to it, I'd like to get started on your defense right away."

Emma was both emotionally and physically drained, but she couldn't rest until she knew they'd gotten the ball rolling on her defense. "Could I just have something to eat first?" she asked timidly. She'd been given a tray while she was in custody, but the idea of food had repulsed her.

"We'll order in a sandwich," Elizabeth replied. She glanced at the others. "I'm taking Emma back to my office in my car. Someone can pick her up later."

"Can't Brandon come with us?" Emma asked. "We were together the night of the murder and I have no secrets from him." Except one. She bit her lip. It would probably be a good idea to tell her attorney about Lexine, but she wasn't going to do it in front of him.

"Good idea. That work for you, Mr. Harper?"

"I'm completely at your disposal," he said fervently. His support was what Emma needed the most and she prayed he wouldn't lose faith in her. When they'd shown him in to see her earlier, she had realized how desperately she'd been hoping he would come. Only sheer willpower had enabled her to keep her tears at bay during their brief meeting.

Elizabeth drove Emma while Brandon followed. "Whatever you tell me had better be the truth. I don't like surprises," Elizabeth said as she turned into the alley behind an elegant redbrick building a few blocks from the courthouse and parked in a space marked with her last name. "And I don't like going to trial with my hands tied, so I'll want to know everything, even the details you think are irrelevant. I'll decide what's significant and what isn't."

"I understand," Emma replied. After they got out of Elizabeth's car, a sporty red coupe with fancy chrome wheels and leather interior, Brandon joined them and grasped Emma's hand. They both followed the older woman through the carved double doors of the building.

In the lobby, the glow from a crystal-and-brass chandelier that hung from the high ceiling was reflected in the satin finish of the dark wood walls. The floor was intricately pieced parquet. Their footsteps echoed when they crossed it.

Elizabeth led the way down the hall carpeted in charcoal. Her name in plain gold letters was on the door to her office, next to a long window of beveled glass.

"This is my assistant, Stella Jones," Elizabeth said when they'd gone inside.

An attractive woman with a cloud of curly black hair and deeply tanned skin looked up from her computer terminal and smiled. Gold hoops danced at her ears. As Elizabeth introduced them in turn, Emma and Brandon shook her hand, adorned with a ring on each finger and long dark red nails.

"Let me a have a 'new client' form and we'll need sandwiches and coffee right away," Elizabeth told

her. "Call Corwin in the D.A.'s office. I want whatever he's got on the Christina Montgomery murder
case. Send Jody over." Stella was writing quickly.
"Corwin will be pouting, since I beat down his bail
denial, but just ignore him. He owes me a favor."
Elizabeth finally took a breath. "Any messages?"

"Nothing urgent. They're on your voice mail."
Stella handed her some papers. "Turkey sandwiches
okay?" she asked them all.

To Emma that sounded heavenly. She felt hollow
and shaky.

"I'll bring coffee in a minute." Stella reached for
the phone.

"Best assistant I ever had," Elizabeth said as she
led the way past a room lined with legal tomes. "I
stole her away from my late husband."

"Was he an attorney, too?" Emma asked.

Elizabeth glanced over her shoulder. "The best."

They entered her office, carpeted in the same thick
charcoal as the hallway. The chairs she indicated were
covered in a teal-and-burgundy plaid and her desk
was an elegant antique in some exotic wood that
Emma didn't recognize. The wall behind Elizabeth's
leather chair was covered with awards and certifi-
cates. Beneath the window was a low bookcase, on
the other wall a sideboard in the same wood as the
desk. Over it was a grouping of framed aerial photos.

"Were those taken by a friend of yours?" Brandon
asked while Emma studied a shot of the mountains.

Elizabeth sat down and folded her hands together.
"My husband took those."

"He was a pilot?" Emma asked.

"No, I'm the pilot. Sometimes commuting by air is the only way I can stay on schedule. Besides my practice here in Whitehorn, I teach and I also do some legal commentating for one of the networks."

She handed Emma the blank forms. "Take these home with you and fill them out," she said. "It's all routine information." She slid open a drawer and took out a legal pad, then she set up a tape recorder. "Okay, let's get to work," she said as she uncapped an elegant gold pen. "Give me your phone number first."

As Emma complied, the door opened behind her. Stella brought in a silver tray that she set on the sideboard. Asking their preferences, she served the coffee in elegant china cups and then slipped from the room.

Emma sipped the strong, hot brew, as did Brandon. Elizabeth ignored the cup Stella had placed at her elbow. Instead she fixed a level gaze on Emma.

"Truth time," she said. "Your blood was found at the crime scene. How do you explain that?"

For a moment Emma simply stared, her mind a blank. "I can't," she said finally. "I've never been in the woods."

Elizabeth's blue eyes narrowed. "Remember what I told you. Don't jerk me around."

"I'm not!" Emma cried, her eyes filling with fresh tears. "It's the truth."

Elizabeth stared while Emma tried not to fidget. She'd racked her brain trying to figure out how her blood could have gotten anywhere near Christina, but she'd come up with nothing.

"I don't know," she wailed, shaking her head. "I haven't got an explanation because there isn't one!"

Brandon reached over to pat her hand. "It's okay, baby. We'll figure this out."

Elizabeth sat back in her chair, finally picking up the delicate china cup and drinking her coffee. A tiny frown formed a pleat between her brows as she continued to study Emma over the brim.

There was a knock on the door and Stella came in again. This time the silver tray held plates of sandwiches and chips.

Once Stella had served her, Emma stared at the food and realized her appetite had fled once again.

"Is there anything else I can get you?" Stella asked.

After glancing at the others, Elizabeth thanked her and sent her away.

"Let's take a break from this," she said, waving her fingers over the yellow pad.

For the next few minutes they chatted as they ate. Brandon asked Elizabeth about flying. They discussed the relative merits of different planes while Emma concentrated on chewing and swallowing each bite of the sandwich that tasted like cardboard and stuck in her throat like glue. When she'd managed to down half of it, Elizabeth pounced.

"Let's go back to the beginning. Tell me a little about your childhood and then bring me up to last August."

Emma looked at Brandon, who smiled his encouragement, and then she recited the basic facts of her life. As soon as she mentioned being abandoned as a baby, Elizabeth leaned forward.

"You weren't in contact with your birth mother?"

The lie nearly stuck in Emma's throat. "No. I actually came here to find her."

Elizabeth shoved back her chair and got to her feet. "Emma, is it possible that you had a twin?" Excitement vibrated in her voice as she leaned down and braced her hands on the desktop.

"What are you getting at?" Brandon asked. "What difference would that make?"

"Identical twins share the same DNA," she replied.

A chill slid down Emma's spine. Wouldn't she know if she had a twin? Even separated, surely they'd share some kind of cosmic link. The idea that she might have a double out there and not even know it was ludicrous.

"That's not possible!" she exclaimed.

Brandon had turned in his chair. "Sure it is, honey. It's one explanation for this mess you're in."

Emma worried her lower lip with her teeth. She didn't know the answer to Elizabeth's question, but someone else did.

Lexine! Would she have admitted to Emma that she had a sister? Maybe not.

"What is it?" Elizabeth demanded. "Do you remember something?"

How Emma hated hurting Brandon's feelings, especially when he'd been so supportive, so unwavering in his belief that she was innocent. "Would you mind if I talked to Elizabeth alone?" she asked reluctantly.

For a moment he looked stunned. Then a shutter dropped down over his face and he shoved back his chair. Only the bright splotches of color on his cheekbones betrayed whatever emotion he must be feeling as he stood.

"No problem. I'll wait outside." His gaze was averted as he headed for the door.

"I'm sorry," Emma whispered, but he didn't seem to hear her.

"Okay," Elizabeth said the moment the door had closed behind him. "What's up?"

Emma laced her fingers together and stared at them. The half sandwich she'd managed to eat sat like lead in her stomach and her nerves were stretched as tight as a bungie cord. What would her attorney think when she learned that Emma, whose innocence must appear so very unlikely, was related by blood to a woman who had killed not once, but three times?

Would she withdraw from Emma's case?

"I'm waiting." Elizabeth sounded exactly like a teacher quizzing a student.

Emma barely stopped herself from squirming in her chair. She took a deep breath and told the other woman about her mother.

"Wow," Elizabeth said when she was done. "I hope the press doesn't get hold of this."

A wave of new anxiety crashed into Emma. "Me, too."

"Do you think she'd tell you the truth if you asked?" Elizabeth had sat down and was scribbling notes to herself.

"I have no idea." The admission was a difficult one for Emma to make, but she had to be realistic. The sheriff had told her that when he'd gone to visit Lexine she had tried to implicate Emma.

To divert suspicion from someone else...

Emma sat up straighter in her chair as the realization hit her. Before she could say anything, there was a soft knock on the door. Brandon?

Stella poked her head inside. "Jody brought this back from the D.A.'s office," she said, handing a manila envelope to Elizabeth. "Corwin said to call him in the morning."

"Thanks," Elizabeth replied absently as Stella picked up the sandwich plates. Once the door was shut again, Elizabeth laid down the envelope and looked expectantly at Emma. "What is it?"

Emma told her about the sheriff's visit to the prison. "He's my half brother," she added. "Lexine abandoned him, too."

Elizabeth shook her head. "As a mother and a grandmother, I can't even begin to understand what motivates that kind of woman." She opened the envelope and pulled out a folder. "Give me a minute to look this over."

Emma got to her feet. She was stiff from sitting for so long. "I'll go see if Brandon is still here."

"You haven't told him about your connection to this woman?" Elizabeth asked.

Emma shook her head. "Two of her victims were members of his family."

"That's a tough one, but it's obvious he cares about you, and he's bound to find out. It might be easier coming from you." When Emma didn't reply, she shrugged. "Secrets are like infections," she said in her characteristic blunt way. "Left untreated, they fester. Think about it. When you come back, you can bring him with you if you want," she said. "Unless you'd rather not." She returned her attention to the papers in front of her and Emma slipped from the room.

When she walked out to the reception area and saw that Stella was alone, her heart sank. She'd hoped he might stick around even though she'd hurt his feelings.

Stella glanced up from her terminal. "If you're looking for Mr. Harper, he went outside to use his cell phone."

Relief hit Emma so hard she thought her knees would buckle. She was dangerously close to emotional overload, but she needed to know that he hadn't completely given up on her.

When she went outside, she saw him standing with his back to her and his hands jammed into the pockets of his suit pants. The sky was overcast, but the temperature was mild and Emma was warm enough in the windbreaker she had on over her shirt and pants.

She'd barely noticed before how handsome Brandon looked in his elegant gray suit, but now she did. For a moment she watched him unobserved. His jacket fit smoothly across his broad shoulders and his slacks followed the lean length of his legs. He must have sensed her presence, because he turned around with an aloof expression.

"All through?" he asked. A dozen feet separated them, but he didn't move.

"She's going over what she got from the district attorney. Would you like to rejoin us now?"

For a moment Emma feared he was going to make a sarcastic comment, but finally the tension went out of his shoulders and he closed the gap between them. He didn't touch her, though, and she felt the loss like a cold wind.

"I'd like that," was all he said.

"Brandon—" Frustrated, she stopped, conscious of the lack of time to explain and her own indecision. What if her news sent him back to Reno? Now more than ever she needed his support.

"What is it?" Curiosity gleamed in his blue eyes.

Emma had no choice but to bide her time. "I'm glad you're here," she said simply, ignoring the relief her rationalizing brought with it.

His smile, when it finally came, warmed her to her toes. "Me, too." With her hand tucked in his, they went inside together.

Brandon followed Emma back into the office, still curious about what she hadn't been able to discuss with her attorney in front of him. While he'd been waiting outside, he'd called Garrett to update him. When the old man asked if Brandon's faith in Emma could possibly be misplaced, he'd damn near bit off his tongue to keep from taking his frustration out on the old man. Was it possible, as Garrett suggested, that Brandon had been listening to his libido instead of his head? Not that *libido* was the term Garrett had used.

No, Brandon had always gone with his gut and followed his instincts, both when it came to business and with people. That was one reason he was so successful. While the next guy was still thinking a deal through, weighing the pros and cons, Brandon had already acted on it.

Right now every instinct he had was telling him he was right to believe in Emma. Whatever he was using to do his thinking with, it insisted he stick by her.

Once he'd held out her chair and then seated himself, Elizabeth opened the folder in front of her and slid a colored photo across the desktop. "Recognize this?"

It was a picture of a gold locket. The chain was broken and part of it appeared to be tarnished.

Emma examined the photo carefully. "It's pretty ordinary, but I don't remember it. Whose is it?"

"The police think the killer might have dropped it. They found it near the body, but her brother didn't recognize it and the blood on the chain isn't Christina's."

Emma paled. "So the killer really might be a woman. Is that where the blood sample came from?"

"From that and the victim's fingernails."

"I don't remember reading anything about a

locket,'' Brandon mused. He'd looked up some articles about the murder after Emma had first been questioned.

Elizabeth raised her brows. "Right again. The police didn't release that information." She took back the photo. "The other curious thing about the locket is there was a partial fingerprint on it. The police weren't able to match it to Christina. You've convinced me it won't match your prints, either."

Emma frowned. "If I do have a twin, wouldn't our fingerprints be identical as well as our DNA?"

A smile spread slowly across Elizabeth's face. "No, they wouldn't. While we run down Emma's birth certificate, I think we'll have the lab run another test."

"What's the point?" Brandon asked impatiently. "We've been through this before."

Elizabeth tapped her pen on the desk, her smile growing even wider. "In one of my recent cases, I had reason to study this. Even with identical twins, there can be markers in the DNA that don't match. That's what we'll have them look for. While we're at it, we'll have some other tests run." Her glance strayed to Emma's hair. "They found trace evidence in the victim's car, including some fiber samples and a few strands of hair. Did you happen to go blond last year?"

"No," Emma replied, tucking a stray lock behind her ear. "I've never colored my hair."

"Good." Elizabeth read down the page in front of her. "What size shoe do you wear?"

"A seven," Emma replied. "Did they find footprints?"

"Mmm-hmm. Some from Christina's shoes along with prints from a hiking boot small enough to belong either to a woman or a teenage boy. Too bad your feet aren't bigger, but this does go along with the possible twin theory. The reason they eliminated Homer Gilmore as a suspect after they found him with Christina's license plate is because he has huge feet."

"I wondered why they let him go," Brandon muttered.

Elizabeth closed the file and glanced at her slim gold watch. "I'll arrange for your blood test in the morning."

"How long will the results take this time?" Brandon asked. How big a toll would waiting take on Emma?

"Don't worry. I'm not a small-town police department. We'll hear back in a day or two. Meanwhile, unless either of you has any questions, let's call it a day." She gave Emma a sympathetic glance. "Get some rest." She jotted a number on the back of her business card and handed it to Emma. "Call me if you need anything. Stella always knows where I am and I'm never without my cell phone." She extended her hand, first to Emma and then to Brandon.

"Thank you for helping me," Emma murmured.

Brandon added his thanks to hers. He was still curious about what the two of them had discussed without him. Would Emma tell him?

"I haven't helped you yet," Elizabeth said, "but

we'll get to the bottom of this. Meanwhile, you might see that she takes care of herself,'' she told Brandon.

Although he understood she was giving him something to do to keep him busy, he welcomed the task. ''I'll watch her like a hawk,'' he vowed.

Moments later, as he and Emma were walking back to his car, he blew out a long breath. ''How are you holding up?'' he asked. ''Are you hungry?''

She shook her head. ''I'd just like to go back to the ranch, if that's okay with you.''

The idea of having her in his bed again tonight sent desire surging through him. He tried to ignore it, but the need to reassert his claim was strong.

Damn, the last thing she should have to cope with was him crawling all over her. ''I'll bring you back to the lab in the morning,'' he offered as he unlocked the passenger door of the Lexus.

Emma hesitated. ''Uh, would you drop me off at my apartment instead. I can take my own car.''

''I don't mind going with you.'' Did she think he was letting her face any of this ordeal alone?

She ran a hand through her hair as her gaze slid away from his. ''That's okay, really. I know you must have other things you need to do.''

Was he being dismissed? Just because he was sleeping with Emma didn't mean she had to tell him everything, he reminded himself. It was obvious that when it came to their relationship, they weren't on the same page.

He opened her car door wider. ''No problem.'' He thought he saw a flash of anguish on her face before she got into the car, but he couldn't be sure. Well, hell, she had plenty to be upset about without him adding to her stress.

Determined to not pressure her, he climbed in behind the wheel. As soon as he did, she leaned over and gave him a kiss on the cheek. "I'm sorry," she murmured.

Immediately he turned his head so his mouth meshed with hers. He buried his fingers in her hair and held her head still. "There's nothing for you to be sorry for," he replied after he'd forced himself to let her go.

As he turned the key in the ignition, he could have sworn he heard her whisper, "I wish that was true."

Ten

It had been a long three days since Emma's arrest and her subsequent release on bail. Despite Melissa's reservations, Janie had insisted that Emma come back to work at the café. Staying busy helped move the hours along as she waited to hear from her attorney.

Last night Emma had insisted on coming back to her apartment. As much as she enjoyed staying at the ranch, it was time to reclaim her own life. The reporters, in search of other stories, were gone from her driveway when she arrived. Today as the slightly larger than usual lunch crowd finally tapered off, she took a moment to reminisce about the way she and Brandon had spent the early hours of the morning together in her bed. When she was with him, she almost forgot the sword hanging over her head.

Now she noticed a stranger at the counter watching her. His gaze shifted quickly and she wondered whether he was a reporter or just someone who wanted a good look at a criminal. She was tempted to offer him her autograph. Maybe she could sell them and put the money into her defense fund. She was going to owe Brandon a lot of money when this was over, but she was determined to pay him back every dime.

Although she was getting used to being gawked at and whispered about, it was exhausting to have to guard her every word and expression for fear it might be judged—or quoted in the morning newspaper. If she laughed, was she heartless? If she smiled, had she no remorse?

Yesterday she'd been taking an order when the customer, a woman Emma had never seen in town before, suddenly whipped out a tape recorder and asked if Emma was allowed to handle knives from the kitchen.

"Christina wasn't stabbed," she'd retorted before she could stop herself. "She was hit over the head. Aren't you going to ask if I'm allowed to lift anything heavy?"

This morning a customer brought in a scandal rag bearing the headline, Suspect Admits Bashing Victim with Soup Pot. A little later, Elizabeth's assistant had phoned Emma at the café and reminded her to keep her mouth shut.

"Elizabeth said to tell you we haven't been able to run down a copy of your birth certificate yet, but that we expect to hear back on the DNA test either today or tomorrow, so we'll be in touch."

The hours since then had dragged, and Brandon had come by the Hip Hop twice this morning to ask if she'd heard anything. It was a miracle Emma could keep her orders straight.

It was a miracle he was still standing by her. Two days ago, after he'd brought her back to her car, Emma had insisted on driving herself out to the prison to see Lexine. Not that she had admitted to Brandon where she was headed.

Her stomach had twisted itself into a knot of apprehension as she waited, hoping Lexine might shed some light on the circumstances surrounding Emma's birth. But the ordeal had been for nothing. Lexine had angrily denied having twins. She'd become so infuriated by Emma's question that it had taken two guards to remove her from the visitors' room.

Although Emma had been humiliated by Lexine's outburst and deeply disappointed by the mission's failure, Elizabeth remained optimistic. She had advised Emma to forget about that and focus instead on the fingerprint expert's inability to link her to the partial print on the locket.

"How are you doing?" Janie asked now as Emma stared unseeingly at the blackboard where the daily specials were posted. Although being married to a deputy put Janie in a potentially awkward position, she'd made it clear to anyone willing to listen that she believed in Emma's innocence. That was more than Rafe had done; except for a brief message on her machine asking how she was and piquing Brandon's curiosity, he was keeping his distance.

Emma was just about to ask Janie if she could take a break when the bell over the front door jangled. Both women glanced around to see how many new arrivals had come in.

Emma's heart climbed right into her throat when she saw Elizabeth standing in the entry surveying the room. Today her neatly tailored suit was forest green and her tasteful jewelry was gold.

Mingled hope, fear and denial all warred within Emma as her attorney's gaze finally met hers. Emma's knees wobbled uncontrollably and her feet were glued to the floor. Was it a good sign that Elizabeth had come in person, or a bad one? As Emma stared, afraid even to breathe or blink, Elizabeth stuck out her fist.

Her thumb was upraised in an unmistakable gesture of approval and triumph.

Janie let out a shriek that nearly stopped Emma's heart and then the other waitress grabbed her around the waist. Earlier Emma had confided in them that she was waiting for the new test results.

As Charlene and the cook burst out of the kitchen to see what the commotion was, Elizabeth came over to where Emma stood trembling with relief.

"Corwin's dropping the charges," she said without bothering to lower her voice. "The person whose blood was on the locket never had a rubella vaccination and your sample shows unmistakably that you did."

Emma was frozen in place, hardly daring to believe the nightmare could really be over. "Was that enough to convince him?"

"Without a shred of evidence to place you at the scene, he realized he had no case." Elizabeth looked smug. "Even Corwin realizes that going to trial with nothing more than an eyewitness who sees UFOs and a telephone tip from an anonymous source would be a bit of a mistake." She picked an invisible speck off her sleeve. "His office is drawing up the paperwork as we speak."

"I'm free?" Emma whispered.

Elizabeth's smile deepened the lines around her mouth and eyes. "Yes, Emma, now you're officially free."

Without thinking, Emma flung her arms around her attorney's neck. "Thank you!"

Chuckling, Elizabeth patted her back. "You're very welcome."

Embarrassed by her impulsiveness, Emma let the other woman go. As she did, realization hit and she pulled Elizabeth aside.

"This means that you were right," Emma whispered, her voice laced with horror. "I do have a twin sister, and she might be a murderer."

"Don't think about that," Elizabeth replied quietly. "If that proves to be true, then she is no more connected to you than Lexine is."

"She's my twin," Emma muttered. "Identical in every way."

"No!" Elizabeth insisted. "Not identical. Her DNA is different, her fingerprints are different, and her character is vastly different from yours. She's a stranger, one willing to let you take the heat for something she very probably did."

Slowly the attorney's words penetrated the haze of disappointment surrounding Emma like a cloud. She hadn't thought of it that way. "Maybe she would have come forward eventually."

Elizabeth gripped Emma's upper arms and looked straight into her eyes. "Don't count on it. She's not you."

Emma swallowed. "I suppose you're right."

"Of course I am," Elizabeth drawled. "Now I'd imagine there are a couple of phone calls you'd like to make," she reminded Emma. "And I'm meeting Garrett Kincaid for a late lunch."

"Brandon!" Emma exclaimed. "I have to call Brandon."

"Don't forget your parents." Elizabeth's voice was dry. "I'm sure they'd appreciate hearing they won't have to visit you in jail."

Emma smiled sheepishly. She'd called them very reluctantly the evening of the day she'd made bail. They'd wanted to come right out, but she had managed to persuade them to hold off. "I'll call them first," she promised.

Elizabeth looked at her watch. "I'd better run— I'm due in court—but I do enjoy delivering good news in person." After Emma thanked her again, she hurried away.

"Use the phone in Melissa's office," Janie suggested generously. "Under the circumstances, I don't think she'd mind."

Janie didn't have to make the suggestion twice. As Emma hurried across the café, she was astonished at the number of people who'd overheard the news and wanted to offer their congratulations. Finally, as her face started aching from the wide smile she couldn't suppress, she reached the office. Shutting the door behind her, she sat at Melissa's desk and burst into tears.

Garrett hadn't been this attracted to a woman since his beloved Laura had died after fifty wonderful years together.

"What's next on your calendar?" he asked Elizabeth, who was seated across from him at Whitehorn's only authentic English tearoom. Their lunch had gotten off to a festive beginning with her announcement about Emma. Garrett was pleased to hear that Brandon's faith in her hadn't been misplaced. In the game of love, the boy could do a darn sight worse than a sweet woman who clearly adored him.

Always priding himself on his ability to think on his feet, Garrett had taken the opportunity to give Elizabeth a congratulatory hug. To his surprise, she'd seemed no more eager to end the impromptu embrace than he'd been. In fact, her reluctance, as well as the way her attention seemed riveted on him throughout their meal, had prompted his last question.

"Actually, I do have a gap in my schedule," she admitted now, the corners of her mouth turning up in the most delightful way. "Another case has been postponed for the prosecutor's hernia surgery and a television show I was consulting on has been canceled by the network." She stunned Garrett by fluttering her lashes provocatively. "Why do you ask?"

Her hand, adorned only by a thin gold ring set with diamonds, lay on the table. Garrett summoned his courage and covered it with his. The contrast between her soft translucent skin and his, as tough and tanned as old leather, wasn't lost on him. Neither was the spark he felt at her touch when she turned her hand over and linked her fingers with his.

"I wondered if you'd be interested in visiting the ranch," he said after he'd swallowed the wad of nerves in his throat. "It's real pretty this time of year and you could stay as long as you like."

Her eyes widened in surprise and he cursed himself silently for being such a fool. She was brilliant, educated and famous, everything he wasn't. What would she—

"I'd love that," she said, shocking the bejesus out of him.

As he gaped, unable to hide his astonished pleasure, she picked up her cup, as delicate as an eggshell, and took a sip of her tea. Above the rim, her eyes danced with warm laughter.

"Well, that's fine," he managed to say, feeling as gauche as an inexperienced schoolboy. "How soon can you come?"

She set her cup back in the saucer and leaned forward. "How soon do you want me?"

At the prison, Audra stared anxiously through the partition at Lexine, whose face had gone purple with rage. Audra had come out the minute she'd heard on the radio that all charges against Emma Stover in the murder of Christina Montgomery had been dropped. So much for her mother's brilliant plan to divert any possibility of guilt from Audra, her own flesh and blood.

"Now what are we going to do?" Audra hated the whine in her voice, but was powerless to prevent it. "I'm scared. What if they identify me in some way from that call I made? They'll wonder why I was so eager for them to arrest that waitress. The next thing I know—"

"Will you shut up!" Lexine shouted into the receiver. "I can't think with you wailing in my ear like a damn baby."

Several other people in the visitors' room turned to stare as Audra slid lower in her chair. She shouldn't have come out here. Instead of appreciating all her attention, Lexine acted as though this latest fiasco was all Audra's fault.

As she stared sullenly, resentment eating at her insides like acid, Lexine's frown deepened. "You might as well leave," she said bluntly, waving her hand in dismissal. "Don't come back unless I contact you. I don't want anyone connecting us and starting to wonder if I had some hand in that certain incident you told me about. We'd better both keep a low profile for a while."

Audra opened and closed her mouth a couple of times, but nothing came out. Tears filled her eyes. Lexine *needed* her; she looked forward to these visits from her little girl. They brightened her lonely existence in this awful place. No one cheered her up like Audra did, or so she'd said before asking for cigarettes or nail polish or a magazine.

But now Lexine was cutting Audra off as though her visits meant nothing. Lexine was tossing her away again, just as she had when Audra was a baby.

The old hag was already serving consecutive life sentences for her crimes. What more did she have to lose?

"Why the hell are you crying?" Lexine demanded, her voice like a whip. "I've never seen such a spineless wimp." She looked around carefully and then she lowered her voice. "You get your skinny butt back out there and find that mine," she said through gritted teeth. "If I'm ever going to find a way to buy my way out of here and make the Kincaids pay for putting me here, I need those stones. So if you don't want to find yourself in the next cell, you'd better damn well quit your sniveling and get busy!"

"Mama!" Audra gasped. Was she threatening to tell what she knew?

Lexine sat back in her chair, her expression cold and detached. "Now get out of here. I've got some thinking to do."

After Emma got off the phone with the Stovers back in Clear Brook, she decided she wanted to see the expression on Brandon's face as she told him the good news and thanked him for all his help.

If she didn't quit dawdling, someone else was going to spill the beans. Eagerly she called him on his cell phone. When he answered on the second ring, she breathed a sigh of relief and asked him to meet her at her apartment.

"What's up?" he asked. "I'm out in the pasture in the ranch Jeep," he replied. "It'll take me a half hour to get back to the house."

"I'd just like to see you whenever you can get here." She was barely able to contain her excitement. When he asked if she'd talked to Elizabeth yet, she pretended the signal was cutting out and they were losing the connection.

"If you can hear me, I'll see you at your place in a while," he shouted, clear as day.

Smiling to herself, Emma hung up the phone and glanced at her watch. She'd have enough time to pick up a bottle of champagne, change her clothes and set the scene for a very private celebration.

As she left the office, her smile faded. It was still difficult to believe she had a sister out there somewhere, an identical twin. Still worse was the idea that her twin had apparently followed their mother into a life of crime.

Emma felt as though she had gained and lost a sister in the space of a few moments. Now, more than ever, it was important that she tell Brandon about Lexine.

She refused to let anything ruin their celebration. Time enough later for serious conversation, and for hoping his feelings for her had grown stronger than his loathing for her mother must already be.

When Brandon hurried out the front door of the ranch house, curious about where Garrett had disappeared to that morning, he nearly ran into a man

standing on the porch with his hand poised to ring
the bell.

"Can I help you?" Brandon asked without bothering to hide his impatience. He was in a fever to get
to Emma.

The visitor was casually dressed, but there was
something about his sharp, close-set eyes that alerted
Brandon's survival instincts.

"Are you Brandon Harper, Emma Stover's boyfriend?" the man asked.

Brandon was right. Another reporter. "I have no
comment," he said bluntly. "You're on private property, so I suggest you get your tail in gear before I
kick it down to the main gate."

The man was slightly built and he took a wary step
back as Brandon advanced. "An answer to one question is all I want." His persistence didn't impress
Brandon, who ignored his query, taking his arm instead with the intention of stuffing him back in his
car.

"How do the Kincaids feel about your relationship
with Lexine Baxter's daughter?" he asked as Brandon hustled him down the walk.

"You're nuts." Brandon wrenched open the door
to the nondescript compact. Emma hadn't found her
mother yet.

"You mean, you didn't know?" the reporter
yelped, jerking his arm from Brandon's grasp.

"You'd better fire your sources," Brandon snarled,
grabbing for him again.

"She didn't tell you she's been to the women's

prison twice to visit Lexine?'' the little man said,
dancing away from Brandon's reach. ''She was there
two days ago.'' Taking a piece of paper from his
pocket, he unfolded it and shoved it in Brandon's
face. ''Look at this, if you don't believe me. It's a
copy of the sign-in log from the prison. There's her
name.''

Brandon hesitated. Could that have been one of the
errands Emma had insisted on running by herself? He
grabbed the form, recognizing her signature high-
lighted in bright yellow.

His stomach clenched. Why hadn't she told him?
''Where did you get this?'' he demanded.

''I have my sources.'' The reporter retrieved the
paper from Brandon's numb fingers. ''Tell me, Mr.
Harper,'' he asked in a cheerful voice, ''do you think
the propensity for violence can be passed on from
mother to daughter, like eye color or a good singing
voice? Are you willing to believe now that Emma
Stover is guilty of murder?''

Barely resisting the urge to smash his fist into the
other man's grinning face, Brandon instead shoved
him aside, dug out his keys and stalked to his Lexus.
With the reporter hot on his tail, he headed for town.

The champagne was chilling in the refrigerator and
a bouquet of daisies sat in a pitcher on the kitchen
table. Emma had showered and changed into black
leggings and a teal-blue top with a scoop neckline.
Her hair was loose around her shoulders and she'd
used the perfume her folks had sent for her last birth-

day. A vanilla candle burned on the counter and a George Strait CD played in the background. She'd thought about pulling the bed out and decided that was too obvious.

When she heard a car pull up outside, she checked her reflection in the bathroom mirror, realized she'd forgotten to put on earrings and grabbed the gold hoops that made her feel flirtatious. By the time her trembling hands had them fastened in her ears, footsteps were thudding up the outside staircase.

Before Brandon could knock on the door, Emma threw it open. She was near to bursting with excitement.

"Rafe!" Emma's face fell like a failed soufflé.

He must have seen her disappointment before she could hide it. "I guess this isn't for me," he said, with an all-encompassing gesture. "You look terrific, by the way. Am I interrupting?"

"Brandon's coming over," she replied warily. Hadn't Sheriff Rawlings gotten the news?

"I won't stay, but I heard about the charges being dropped and I wanted to pass on my congratulations." A smile softened his harsh expression. "I'm glad for you, Emma."

His obvious sincerity caught her completely by surprise. "Oh, don't make me cry," she wailed, blinking rapidly. "It will ruin my makeup." She held the door open wider. "Would you like to come in?"

He glanced behind him. "Nah, you're expecting Brandon. Does he know yet?"

She shook her head. "I wanted to see his face."

Rafe gave her a searching look. "Have you told him about our mother?"

Emma dropped her gaze to the insignia over his pocket. "No."

Rafe leaned over and lifted her chin with his finger. "If you care about this guy, you'd better tell him before someone else does."

Emma whirled away. "Oh, how can I admit that I'm ashamed of my own mother?" Her gaze flew back to Rafe. Lexine was *his* mother, too. "I'm sorry. I didn't mean—"

"Do you think I'm proud of her?" he challenged. "If Brandon cares as much as I think he does, he'll understand."

In her heart, she knew Rafe was right. *If* Brandon cared. That was the kicker that scared her. Could he love someone like her?

"Thanks," she murmured to Rafe, "and thanks for coming by."

"We'll get together real soon," he promised. "Raeanne, Skye and I, you and Brandon." He enfolded Emma in a big, awkward hug. For a moment she tried to absorb some of his courage and confidence. Just as she stepped back, she saw Brandon's car pulling into the driveway.

Rafe noticed it, too. "I'll talk to you later," he said, turning away.

He met Brandon at the bottom of the stairs as Emma watched with renewed excitement. She couldn't see Rafe's face below the rim of his Stetson, but Brandon's expression when he nodded at the sheriff was unsmiling, even grim.

He was probably worried that the sheriff had come in his official capacity, she realized. He must have been reassured when he saw that Rafe was leaving, his handcuffs still dangling from his belt.

"Hi," she called.

Brandon looked up and she forgot all about Rafe as love swelled inside her like a birthday balloon. His solemn face had grown so dear to her. He was still the most attractive man she had ever met and now that she knew him so well, he appealed to her on many more levels that merely the physical. If only he would open up to her more, but then, who was she to begrudge him his secrets?

"I have good news," she said, unable to wait another minute as he mounted the steps. "Elizabeth got the results from the second DNA test."

Brandon's hand tightened on the railing. His face was taut. "And?"

Happiness fluttered in Emma's chest. "I've been cleared. The charges were dropped."

His stern expression softened as he hurried up the stairs. "I'm glad." His voice was gruff. When he reached the landing, Emma pulled him inside and threw her arms around his neck.

His body felt stiff in her embrace and he only held her for a moment before he set her away. "So, Elizabeth was right? You do have a twin out there somewhere?"

The idea was still difficult for Emma. "A twin who's probably a murderer."

"I'm sorry," Brandon said. "That has to be tough for you. Any idea who or where she is?"

Emma could answer that question truthfully. "No, none. I imagine the sheriff will start looking into it, but there's been some problem finding my birth certificate."

"Speaking of Sheriff Rawlings," Brandon said, standing over Emma as she settled herself on the couch, "why was he here just now?"

Could that be possessiveness she heard in Brandon's voice? Even jealousy?

Emma patted the seat next to her as she smiled up at him, but he ignored the gesture, instead jamming his hands into the pockets of his tan slacks. She'd hoped to delay this discussion until after they'd cracked open the champagne, but she couldn't keep evading the truth.

"Rafe is my half brother," she said with a trace of defiance. "He was only stopping by to congratulate me."

Except for a slight narrowing of his eyes, Brandon's expression didn't change. "Let me see," he drawled, "does that mean you shared the same father, or is Lexine Baxter his mother, too?"

His comment shocked Emma, but she tried her best to not let her reaction show. "That's right." She lifted her chin defiantly. "How long have you known?"

"Not as long as you."

"Who told you?" Emma demanded.

Brandon leaned down, bracing his hand on the arm of the couch, and stared into her face. "The question," he said in a low voice, "is why you weren't the one to tell me. Why have you been pretending that you hadn't yet found her?"

Eleven

"I was going to tell you about Lexine today," Emma said, a guilty flush heating her cheeks.

"Huh." He managed to inject a whole load of disbelief into that one word as he straightened to his full height. "And how long have *you* known about her?"

She bit her lip, unable to meet his gaze. "Since before you came back."

The silence stretched between them, the only sound in the room coming from the CD Emma had put on earlier. "You look so good in love," George Strait sang.

Emma had a feeling that this time, love wasn't going to be enough. To her surprise, the cushion next to her sagged as Brandon sat down.

"Who your birth mother is and what she's done doesn't make any difference to me," he said. "Mine was a stripper who got involved with a married man."

Emma was surprised by his confession. "But did she kill anyone?"

He sighed and took Emma's hand. "Not that I know of."

"Who told you?" she asked again.

He knew what she meant. "A reporter showed up at the ranch just as I was leaving to come here."

It was Emma's turn to leap up. So the news was out. Crossing the room, she switched off the CD player. Then she whirled to face Brandon. "You're just getting to know your relatives," she said, willing her voice to stay steady. "My mother's identity may not matter to you right now, but believe me, it will matter to the Kincaids. It will matter a lot, and eventually it will make a difference to you, as well." She turned and looked out the window. The street was empty, the neighborhood quiet. No one out there knew or cared that she would always remember this as both the best and the worst day of her life.

She heard Brandon get up and she could feel his nearness, but she kept her back to the room. She should have realized their relationship was doomed from the beginning by things they couldn't change. He might say now that it didn't matter, but she knew differently. He was a self-made man who'd overcome his beginnings to become successful, a man with ties to one of Montana's prominent families. In time, if he and Emma kept seeing each other, he'd come to resent her sordid baggage. The smart thing to do was to break off with him now, before she fell any deeper in love.

"Emma," he said, placing his hands on her shoulders and turning her to face him. "I care about you. Right now you're confused and upset. You've just been through a difficult patch, but it's over with. Let it go."

Before he got done talking she was already shaking

her head. He *cared* for her. The bland phrase hurt like the sharpest sword.

"No," she said, pulling away. "I thought we had so much in common, but I was wrong. I think you'd better go." She thought of the celebration she'd planned and nearly lost the control she was hanging on to by a thread. "Please," she added. "You're right, it's been tough and I'm grateful for your help, but now it's over. I just want to forget about everything that's happened and move on."

A muscle jumped in his cheek. "What are you saying?"

Emma swallowed, knowing what she had to do. She'd waited for him before, all those months, not knowing whether she would ever see him again. She couldn't go through that again. It wasn't as though he *loved* her, after all.

She looked him full in the face, struggling to say the words that would send him away. She swallowed. "It just wouldn't work between us," she whispered, her voice ragged. "We're too different. It's not just Lexine, it's everything."

Brandon gave her one last look, brimming with some strong emotion that she couldn't begin to read. Wordlessly he turned and walked out the door.

Emma rushed to the other window and watched him go. Not once did he hesitate or look back. Maybe he was already beginning to realize that she was right. When his car was finally out of sight, she sank down on the couch and buried her face in her hands.

* * *

"I'm sorry to rush off like this," Elizabeth told Garrett, remorse edging her voice as she threw the few things she'd brought with her to the ranch into her bag.

He sat on the bed they'd shared the night before, watching her. One call on her cell phone and she'd shifted from the warm, loving woman he'd begun falling for the moment he first kissed her to this cool professional.

"It's one case," he argued. "Can't you let it go, wait for the next one?" In the two days since she'd come to the ranch, they'd ridden into the low hills, camped out, shared a sleeping bag, talked for hours. They'd connected, or so he'd thought. He hadn't been this happy in years.

Now she looked up with an expression of regret marring her attractive face. "Garrett, he's a United States senator accused of killing his mistress, but I believe he's being railroaded and I want to help him." She leaned over him and kissed his cheek. "Don't pout," she chided gently. "I'll call you."

When he didn't reply, she glanced at her watch. "If the driver gets here in the next ten minutes, I'll just make my flight." She was talking to herself now, as if she'd already left him behind. "Stella's going by my place to pack what I need. Thank goodness I brought my briefcase along with me."

She ducked into the bathroom for one last check as the doorbell sounded. "That's my car," she said as she came back out, zipped up her bag and grabbed her purse. She picked up her briefcase and Garrett carried the tote for her.

"I could have driven you to the airport," he pointed out as he followed her down the hall, her boots clicking against the hardwood floor.

"I don't like prolonged goodbyes." At the door she reached up to kiss the air by his cheek.

Stubbornly he grabbed her, planting a kiss on her mouth, but she kept her lips closed and he could feel the tension humming through her, the shift in her focus. Disgusted by his need, he released her.

In a blur of motion and flurried words, she was gone. He wondered if his goodbye had registered with her or been lost in her instructions to the driver. As Garrett stood looking at the empty road after her limo had driven away, he was surprised to see Brandon's car.

What was he doing back so soon? Garrett had hoped the hastily scrawled note left propped on the kitchen table was an indication that Brandon's relationship with Emma was moving to the next level. Garrett believed in family, in procreation. He'd hoped his grandson would put down roots in Montana, and what better way than leaving his heart here in Whitehorn? Garrett hadn't expected to see him again until the next morning at the earliest.

As Brandon got out of his car alone, Garrett went to the door to find out why he looked anything but happy.

* * *

Brandon had hoped to have the house to himself, that Garrett and Elizabeth would be out riding the range and he'd have time to figure out what the hell had just happened.

"What are you doing here?" Garrett asked as Brandon stomped through the front door. "I thought you were going to see Emma."

The last thing Brandon felt like was twenty questions, but his grandfather had been good to him so he reached for his patience.

"Don't worry," he said over his shoulder as he headed for the kitchen. "I won't cramp your style." He opened the fridge and dug out a cold beer. He held it up to Garrett, who shook his head.

"No, thanks."

"I'm sure Elizabeth told you about Emma." Brandon popped the top on the beer. Then he tipped his head back and poured a third of the can down his throat. Women! Who could figure any of them out?

"She told me." Garrett's voice was flat. "It's great news, but I still don't understand why the two of you aren't celebrating."

Brandon glanced around. Except for their voices, the house was dead quiet. "Where is she?" he asked.

"Emma? How should I know?"

"No, Elizabeth. Is she taking a nap?" He'd barely seen her except at the dinner table, right before she and Granddad had disappeared for the night. When it came to women, the old man was a fast worker. Brandon was tempted to tell him so, but he might be embarrassed, or she might overhear, and then Brandon would be the one who was embarrassed. He drained the beer, tossed the empty into the recycling bin in the pantry and grabbed another full one. Pulling out a kitchen chair, he spun it around and straddled it, resting his arms on the back.

"Elizabeth left a little while ago." Garrett must have changed his mind about the beer, because he grabbed the rest of the six-pack, dumped some pretzels into a bowl and joined Brandon at the table. Freeing one can from its plastic harness, he stuck his feet out in front of him, worn boots crossed at the ankles, and stared down at them with a barely perceptible sigh.

"Fine lot we are," Brandon said eventually, tapping his beer against Garrett's in an offhand toast. "I thought you two were getting along pretty well. What happened to her?"

"She got a call from Washington," Garrett replied. "Some senator killed his mistress, so Elizabeth rode off into the sunset to save him."

Brandon took a swallow and wiped his mouth with the back of his hand. "Technically that would be sunrise."

"Huh?" Garrett gave him a puzzled frown.

"She went east," Brandon pointed out, sorry he'd brought it up. "The sun sets in the west."

Comprehension dawned. "Well, whichever way she went, she's still gone." His voice was glum, his age evident in the tired lines of his face.

"What about Emma?" Garrett asked before he took a long drink.

Brandon grabbed a handful of pretzels. Between bites he told Garrett about Lexine Baxter.

"Poor Emma," was all he said. Apparently her relationship to the murderer didn't matter much to him. "Now what?"

Brandon shrugged. "Now nothing. To Emma I'm part of the whole sorry mess she wants to forget."

"You gonna let it go at that?" Garrett asked.

"I don't see that I have a choice."

He didn't like the way the old man snorted. "Then I guess you don't. How soon are you leaving for Reno?"

Emma didn't feel like celebrating, but neither did she have the heart to spoil Janie and Charlene's fun when they'd gone to so much trouble. Even Melissa had gotten into the act, offering the café for an open house victory reception during lunchtime on Saturday and providing a huge sheet cake with Free At Last scrawled in red icing.

Since her breakup with Brandon, Emma hadn't been sleeping well. Not only was she more tired than usual, but she must have caught a bug while her resistance was down. She woke up the morning of the party with an upset stomach. Luckily it went away while she was getting ready to leave her apartment.

As she circulated among the crowd of well-wishers at the café, Emma felt strange being out of uniform. In an attempt to at least appear festive, she'd donned a flowered broomstick skirt and a knit T-shirt in bright yellow. Although her face felt stiff from smiling, she was pleased that so many people had come by to offer their congratulations and to have a piece of cake.

A banner hung over the entryway. Balloons and crepe paper streamers decorated the room, and flowers surrounded the table where the cake was displayed. The first thing Emma had done when she arrived was to thank Janie and Charlene for all their work.

Emma had just shaken hands with an older couple, regular café customers, when she turned to see Rafe come in with his wife and daughter. It was the first time Emma had seen him out of uniform. He looked far less intimidating in faded black jeans and a striped shirt.

Grinning, he came straight over to Emma, gave her a brief hug and then introduced Raeanne and Skye. When Skye addressed her as "Aunt Emma," it brought home to her that she had other family here besides a murdering mother and an unknown twin.

"It's so nice to meet you both," Emma said sincerely.

"It's great to see the justice system working the way it was meant to," Raeanne replied with a meaningful glance at her husband. "I've been wanting to have you over for dinner, but I've been swamped at work and then Skye had a cold. She's better now."

Rafe scooped the little girl onto his wide shoulders and she beamed down at Emma from her perch.

"Anyway," Raeanne continued, "any chance you're free Sunday?

"I'd love that," Emma replied. Although she

hadn't come to a decision whether to stay in White-horn or to move on, getting to know the Rawlings was something she looked forward to. While Raeanne gave her directions, Rafe took Skye over to check out the refreshments.

"Oh, dear," Raeanne murmured as the bell over the door sounded and both women looked up. "Have you met Max Montgomery? He's Christina's brother. I feel so sorry for the poor man."

"I've seen him in here, but I didn't know who he was," Emma replied as she studied him curiously.

Max Montgomery reminded her slightly of Brandon. He had black hair and chiseled features, and success clung to him like the well-tailored suit he wore despite the fact that it was Saturday. His expression was closed, his face lined with pain. With a chilly nod at Emma and Raeanne, he went directly to the table in the center of the room, where he picked up a glass and clinked a knife against it.

Conversation faltered as everyone looked around expectantly.

"If I may have your attention for a moment," he said in a commanding voice. "I don't mean to detract from Miss Stover's celebration, but my sister's killer is still at large. That's why I've decided to offer a reward for information leading to his or her arrest and conviction."

People turned to each other and a hum of voices rose through the room.

Montgomery raised his voice, naming a sum that

brought audible gasps from Emma and several other people.

Raeanne groaned. "Rafe won't be happy about this," she predicted as Montgomery thanked the crowd for their attention. Immediately he was circled by a group of people asking questions.

"Won't a reward help with new leads?" Emma asked Raeanne.

"Possibly, but it will also bring in a rash of false clues," she replied. "Greed brings out strange things in people."

Emma hadn't thought about it that way. Before she could comment, Raeanne glanced over her shoulder. "Emma, would you excuse me?" she asked. "I see someone I should speak to." She indicated a pretty redhead standing by herself watching Max Montgomery. "That's Samantha Carter. She's a nurse and an excellent physical therapist. I wanted to get her business card for a friend."

Before Raeanne could leave, the woman she'd indicated saw her and came over.

Raeanne introduced her to Emma.

"Congratulations," Samantha said with a friendly smile. "I don't think I've ever been to a party to celebrate being cleared of murder before."

"And I hope I never do again," Emma replied. "Be sure to have some cake while you're here."

"Thanks, but what I'd really like is to know the identity of the guy who posted the reward."

Raeanne filled her in. "He took his sister's death hard," she added. "I don't think he's going to feel any real closure until her killer is caught and convicted.''

''Poor man,'' Samantha murmured. ''I hope he finds what he's looking for.''

After Raeanne got Samantha's business card, someone called her name and she excused herself.

''I'd better find out what Rafe and Skye are up to,'' Raeanne told Emma. ''If I don't watch them, they'll both eat too much cake.''

''I'll see you tomorrow,'' Emma replied. The mention of food had brought back the touch of nausea she'd felt earlier. After she had fetched a glass of water and was standing on the sidelines wondering how soon she could leave, she saw the back of a dark head across the room. At first Emma thought it was Max Montgomery talking to Rafe.

When he turned, she recognized Brandon. His gaze collided with hers. She felt like bolting, but there was nowhere to go. Hand tightening on the water glass, she stood her ground and watched as he wove his way through the knots of people.

''Hi.'' His voice was cool, his eyes shuttered.

''I'm surprised to see you here,'' Emma blurted, heart aching at the sight of him. He was wearing black loafers, charcoal slacks and a pearl-gray shirt with an open neck and the sleeves rolled back.

Her hand itched to touch him, to feel his warmth. Instead she smiled brightly. ''You don't look like a cowboy today,'' she said inanely.

''I've neglected my business long enough. I just stopped to say goodbye on my way out of town.''

It took an effort to keep her smile from wavering, but she managed. "When will you be back?" The moment the question slipped out, she could have bitten off her tongue. It seemed as though he was always leaving and she was always asking when he'd return. It shouldn't matter anymore, but it did.

Brandon shrugged. "I have no idea."

"I want you to know that I'm going to pay you back for everything you spent to clear my name," she told him.

"I never expected you to do that." His voice was gruff.

"It will take a while, but I'll make regular payments," she continued as though he hadn't spoken. "I'm thinking about looking for a teaching job for the fall."

His gaze sharpened. "Are you leaving Whitehorn?"

"I don't know yet." She needed to take control of her life and make some plans.

"Elizabeth mentioned meeting your grandfather for lunch," she said, changing the subject deliberately. "Is there something going on between them?"

Brandon sighed. "I guess not. She left for Washington a couple of days ago for a big case there."

"That's too bad. I thought they were attracted to each other."

Brandon's mouth twisted into a grimace. "Sometimes attractions don't work out."

What was Emma supposed to say to that? Was he commenting on his grandfather or on the two of them? How insipid an epitaph to what she'd thought they had.

"Emma!" One of her customers, a blue-haired lady who tipped generously, was advancing on her with arms outstretched.

"I've got to go," Brandon said. His gaze rested on Emma's mouth and reaction sizzled through her, but he merely jammed his hands into his pockets.

"Safe trip," Emma murmured, disappointed. The old lady was waiting expectantly. Without another word, Brandon turned and walked away.

"What a nice little party," the woman said as Emma tore her gaze from his retreating figure. When the bell over the front door tinkled to signal his departure, she excused herself abruptly and fled to the kitchen, no longer caring what anyone else thought.

Twelve

"Are you going to tell Brandon that you're pregnant?"

Emma had just come out of the rest room stall where she'd been ill for the third morning in a row to find Janie waiting for her with a concerned expression and her arms folded across her chest.

"Who said anything about being pregnant?" Emma bluffed after she'd rinsed out her mouth at the sink. She hadn't gotten around to using a home test yet, but she had all the signs. At Rafe's on Sunday she'd nearly disgraced herself before making it to the bathroom. Brimming with brotherly concern that Emma found sweet, Rafe had insisted on driving her home while Raeanne and Skye followed in their car.

At the time it had been easy to tell them, and herself, that she'd caught some bug. She'd even expressed concern that she might have passed it on to one of them. Back home, she had counted on her fingers as dismay filled her. She'd never wanted to raise a child alone; neither would she consider giving it up. Now it was obvious from Janie's frown that Emma's bluff had run its course.

"I thought you two were doing fine," Janie said. "Brandon has a right to know."

"We broke up," Emma admitted, tears clogging the back of her throat. "Can you imagine what his reaction would be to finding out that a child he'd fathered had Lexine Baxter's blood in its veins?"

Janie straightened away from the doorjamb where she'd been leaning. "I hadn't thought of that." She gave Emma a hug. "Did he break off with you because of Lexine?"

Emma couldn't allow her to place all the blame on Brandon. "Actually it was more complicated than that." She tossed her head. "It would have never worked. We didn't have that much in common."

"Having a child together can become a shared interest," Janie pointed out dryly. "I can't believe Brandon would blame an innocent baby for something that wasn't its fault. Have you seen a doctor?"

Emma shook her head. "Not yet. I've got a kit at home. You've got to promise me you won't tell Brandon," she said instantly. "If I am pregnant, I need some time to figure out what to do."

"He could help you, with money and stuff," Janie argued.

Emma set her jaw stubbornly. "It'll take me years to repay what I already owe him. Promise me."

"Oh, all right." Janie rolled her eyes. "I won't say anything to Brandon." She studied Emma for a moment. "Do you feel well enough to work today? I could call Charlene if you don't."

"It's her day off. I'll manage." In truth, even though her nausea had passed, Emma's feet were like lead weights and she could have slept for a week.

When she wasn't so exhausted, she needed to look at her options.

She hadn't told anyone that she'd gone out to see Lexine again the day before. Now that Emma knew about a twin, she had hoped for a few answers. As on her previous visits, she'd gotten nowhere with Lexine. Frustrated, angry and hurt, Emma finally left.

On the way home she followed an impulse and stopped to see Rafe at his office. When she told him about her visit, his advice had been to cut Lexine out of her life.

When Emma stalled, he'd asked if Lexine was the real reason behind her breakup with Brandon or just a convenient excuse for something more complicated.

At the time Emma had managed a snort of humorless laughter. Hadn't he figured out that having a convict for a mother was anything *but* convenient?

Later that night, when Emma couldn't sleep, she had finally realized the time had come to let go of her dream. After all the years Emma had longed for a warm, loving relationship with the mother who'd given her life, it was ironic that losing Brandon was so much more painful.

Brandon sat on the patio behind his house and watched the sun sink in the west, its vibrant colors reflected in the still water of the swimming pool. An unlit cigar dangled from his fingers and a snifter of his favorite brandy sat neglected next to his cell phone.

There were calls he should make, deals he should

close, but instead he did nothing. In the three weeks since he'd left Montana, his life had gone as flat as the surface of his swimming pool. The financial business that had always excited him with its challenges now failed to hold his interest. It all seemed pointless.

Worse, he who had prided himself on needing no one found that he missed the rough, easy camaraderie of the Kincaids. He even missed his horse.

Who was he kidding? The only one who could fill up the huge hole in his life was Emma, and she was gone. Damned if he could figure out why. He'd been upset that she'd lied to him, but Lexine wasn't the problem, not really. He'd been guilty, too, of not being open. He saw that now.

All Emma's talk about the two of them not having enough in common was a giant smoke screen. Trust was scary; he knew that. Somehow he had to show Emma that they had more in common than she realized. Once he had her attention, he'd make her see they belonged together.

While he toyed with the idea of lighting the cigar one of his investors had given him, the phone rang. He pursed his lips and debated answering. Indecision was new to him. On the last ring, he picked up the phone and punched the button. "Harper here."

"Brandon, it's Rafe. How's it going?"

Brandon had made an effort to stay in touch with Emma's brother. Now they exchanged pleasantries as Brandon fidgeted, wishing Rafe would get to the point. Finally he interrupted an update on the murder case.

"How's Emma doing?" he asked. "Is she okay?"

There was a pause long enough for Brandon to wonder if the signal had been broken.

"I don't think she's feeling well," Rafe said finally.

Brandon sat up straighter. "You mean, she's sick?"

"I guess. We had her over for dinner right after you left. She seemed to be coming down with a bug, but when we had lunch at the café a couple of days ago she still hadn't bounced back. She's awfully pale and she looks a little thin."

"And you waited until now to call me?" Brandon demanded.

"I didn't think you'd be interested," Rafe replied. "Was it the news about Lexine that broke you up?"

"Emma's background doesn't matter to me any more than yours does," Brandon growled. "Unfortunately, Emma wouldn't listen."

"Well, playing big brother is a little new to me," Rafe said, "so make allowances if I'm awkward at it, but how do you feel about Emma?"

"I miss her."

"Is that it?" Rafe persisted.

The answer came to Brandon in a rush. "No, but that's all I'm sharing with you."

Rafe chuckled. "Fair enough, I guess. Got any ideas?"

"First I need to get Emma's attention. Then I can work on making her listen."

"I've got an idea," Rafe replied, "but it's a little extreme."

"Let's hear it." He listened incredulously as Rafe outlined his plan.

"I think you're insane," Brandon said when he was done.

"Maybe so." Rafe chuckled. "But you have to admit it would get her attention."

"Couldn't you just call like a normal brother?" Emma muttered when Rafe walked up to her car. When she'd seen the revolving light on the top of the black-and-white Cherokee, her first thought was that she was exceeding the speed limit. She'd pulled over, kicking herself for not paying better attention, when the sheriff himself had climbed out of the Jeep and approached her. As soon as she saw his grin, she'd known the traffic stop was bogus.

"I thought you'd like to hear the news," Rafe said as he leaned in her window. "Harper's back in town."

Emma stiffened. "You pulled me over to tell me that?" In the weeks since he'd been gone, the intensity of her heartache hadn't faded a bit. She still missed him like crazy, especially now that she knew she was carrying his child. Thank goodness she'd sworn Janie to secrecy! Emma didn't know which would be worse, for Brandon to feel obligated because she was pregnant or for him to reject the child on the basis of its family tree.

Now Rafe straightened with a sheepish expression. "I thought you might like to know."

"Brandon's arrivals and departures are of no concern to me," Emma huffed. If she'd been Pinocchio, her nose would have hit the windshield. It was *because* she was so interested in news about Brandon that she had to reject it.

"I've got to go," she said, her hand on the gearshift.

"It's not his arrival that's so interesting, it's his mode of transportation."

With an exasperated sigh, Emma gave in to her curiosity. "What do you mean?"

"He's driving a ninety-four Taurus."

"He rented a car, so what?"

Now Rafe looked smug. "I ran the plates. The car's in his name." He cleared his throat. "I called an acquaintance at the Reno P.D. Some huge casino complex they were building has gone bankrupt. Guess who was the principal investor?"

Emma gaped. "Not Brandon?" Was it the project he'd mentioned to her? The biggest thing he'd ever undertaken?

Rafe nodded and then his radio crackled to life. He cocked an ear. "I have to run," he said hastily. "I'll talk to you later."

As he turned away, Emma stuck her head out the window. "Next time can the lights!"

She was waiting for a red light a few minutes later, thinking over what Rafe had told her, when she no-

ticed a dusty Taurus parked at the Mini-Mart where
Patty worked. Emma didn't believe in coincidences.
She was about to look away when she saw Brandon
emerge from the store.

What Rafe had told her was true! Maybe the light
would change and Brandon would be spared the humiliation of knowing she'd seen him.

To her chagrin the light remained stubbornly red
until he pulled in behind her. Her green Chevy wasn't
that easy to miss, but she ignored him all the way
back to her apartment, rationalizing that she couldn't
be expected to recognize him in the white Ford. To
her surprise, he pulled into the Austins' driveway
right behind her.

At least it was way too soon for her to be showing.
Emma took a deep breath and got out to face him.

"Brandon!" She feigned surprise. "What are you
doing here?" She didn't comment on his car; she was
too busy drinking in his appearance.

His face was leaner and there were new lines
around his eyes. Strain was evident in his expression.
Emma's heart went out to him in a rush. Had he lost
everything?

"I've leased out the house in Reno," he explained.
"I'll be staying at the ranch for a while."

So it was true. "Don't be discouraged," she
blurted, forgetting all about playing dumb. "You
were successful once, you can do it again."

His eyes narrowed. "Do you really believe in me
that much?"

"Of course," Emma said, stepping closer. "It was never about your money."

Brandon's frown cleared. "It was never about Lexine, either."

Emma froze. "W-what do you mean?"

"You used her as a shield to hide behind, but she wasn't the problem."

The leap from his financial future to Emma's birth mother left her dizzy. Lexine had tried to wipe out his family and now he said it didn't matter?

"I didn't hide behind anything," Emma retorted. "You couldn't handle the truth."

Brandon brought his face closer to hers. "You didn't give me a chance."

"I was afraid," she gulped, suddenly shaking.

"Afraid of what?" His voice had dropped to a whisper, his gaze was intent on hers.

The truth came to Emma in a rush. "Afraid you'd leave me again. Afraid I couldn't hold you, afraid I wouldn't fit into your world and that mine would bore you." She couldn't believe she'd let all that pour out of her.

"Did it ever occur to you that I had fears, too? I've been alone a long time. I didn't know if I could open up enough to hold on to a woman like you."

"'Like me'?" she echoed.

"Warm, loving, generous, willing to share herself both physically and emotionally."

Emma blushed and looked away. "You're strong and protective," she murmured. "You have good instincts."

"But I lost you," he insisted.

"Only because I was afraid. I'm a coward."

He cocked his head. "Sounds like we're both cowards alone. Let's find out how we'd do together."

"What are you saying?" she asked, her voice shaking.

The instincts that had served Brandon so well in business were shouting at him now, urging him to take the next step. He was a man who'd always listened to his instincts. "Marry me," he said, a surge of love threatening to choke him.

Emma's eyes welled with tears. "Do you mean it?"

"I've never meant anything more. We belong together, the two of us against the world."

She took a deep breath. "Actually, you'd better make that the three of us."

He frowned, puzzled, and then he noticed that her hands were pressed against her stomach.

Protectively.

His eyes widened as shock rippled through him. He stared into her anxious face.

"I'm pregnant," she said as he searched for his voice. "I just thought I should tell you before this goes any further."

"Are you okay? Have you seen a doctor?" Worry for her was uppermost in his mind.

"Yes," she said, "and yes. Are you upset?"

"Upset?" he echoed. "Emma, I've never been so happy." It was true. The woman he loved was carrying his child. He caught her into his arms, careful not to crush her. "Please say you'll marry me."

"My background doesn't bother you?" she asked, pulling free.

"Background?" he repeated, puzzled.

"Lexine."

"Do you love me?"

"Oh, yes." Her eyes were misty and a smile curved her lips.

"That's all the background check I need. Now, are you going to marry me or not?" he asked.

"Of course," she cried, smiling through her tears. "And it doesn't matter that you've lost all your money. Rafe told me. We'll do fine. Don't you worry."

Emma had only meant to reassure him, but to her consternation he stiffened. Then he hugged her and she could feel him shaking in her embrace. When he released her, she stared into his face. Had the reminder of his bad luck pushed him over the edge?

To her surprise, he was grinning widely. "I've got a confession to make, too," he said, taking her hands in his. "I didn't lose any money. I'm still rich. Rafe and I cooked this up so you'd talk to me, that's all. Please don't be mad at us."

Emma looked at the Taurus and then back at Brandon. "You pretended to be poor so I'd talk to you?"

He nodded. "Am I forgiven?"

Emma slid her arms around his neck. "No more dumb ideas," she said. "No more keeping things from each other, agreed?"

Brandon bobbed his head. "I promise."

"In that case, I'll marry you," Emma said. "And I won't hold the fact that you haven't lost all your money against you."

"I can't tell you how relieved I am to hear it." Brandon dipped his head and stilled her laughter with a kiss.

MONTANA BRIDES
continues with

RICH, RUGGED…RUTHLESS
by Jennifer Mikels

also on the shelves this month.
Turn the page for an exciting preview…

Rich, Rugged…Ruthless

by

Jennifer Mikels

"A curse on you, Max Montgomery. You'll get yours one day."

Max leaned back in the forest-green wingback chair behind his desk and watched Dwayne Melrose storm from the office. As president of Whitehorn Savings and Loan Bank, Max could have let one of the loan officers handle Melrose, but because he'd once dated Melrose's daughter while in his teens, he'd given the man a personal appointment. What had been the point? He'd known the outcome before Dwayne had arrived.

Annoyed with himself for even considering an extension, Max pushed back from the highly polished cherry desk. It was past banking hours, too late, but tomorrow morning he'd authorize foreclosure on the Melrose Ranch. He couldn't let Melrose's words touch him. The man had signed an agreement with Whitehorn Savings and Loan, and should uphold his part of it.

He knew people viewed him as hard-hearted in business, but he believed in studying financial statements, not listening to sob stories. The bank's success mattered more than his personal popularity.

Standing, he stuffed a statement of the quarterly

budget into his briefcase and shut it. He viewed himself as pragmatic, perhaps demanding. He had lived the life of one who'd been indulged, who was used to people doing as he said. From the time he was a little boy, he'd had servants catering to his needs. That was part of life as Ellis and Deidre Montgomery's son. As a child, he'd had the finest schooling, and as a man, he'd worked hard for his own success.

With a glance at the digital clock on his desk, he grimaced. He was going to arrive late for his father's political speech to a rangers group in Bozeman. Ellis expected him to come. Rachel, too, had probably received barked orders to make an appearance. Having his grown children in attendance presented the right image. Ellis wanted to be governor so badly he couldn't think about anything else.

Max stepped out of his office, nodded to Edna Redden, his personal assistant, stationed at her desk, but without a word he passed by. He knew she was widowed, had two married children and a grandson. By choice he knew nothing else about her. He kept his distance from her—from everyone.

Beneath a darkening sky, he climbed into his gleaming, black BMW and headed down the town's main street. In passing, he noticed the Hip Hop was jammed. It was fried chicken night, a crowd pleaser. He'd gone a few times, sat alone at the counter and read the newspaper, but talked to no one. It made sense not to make friendships. As the bank's president, he held the purse strings to a lot of people's dreams.

Because he was running late, before reaching the edge of town, he decided to shortcut down an unpaved road that bisected the woods and cut twenty minutes from traveling time. Within half an hour, his car's headlights beamed on the dark road. He didn't need light to know exactly where he was. As if the car had a will of its own, he found himself slowing it at a certain curve. He stared at the woods and in the direction of the rocky embankment where his youngest sister had died.

During those last seconds, had Christina been afraid? Or had her last seconds passed without her being aware someone was behind her with a shovel raised over her head, that danger was near? He hoped for that. He hoped she hadn't been frightened.

Years ago when they'd been closer, he remembered how scared she'd been of a spider that had floated down from a barn rafter and nearly landed on her shoulder. How old had she been? Three. Maybe four, he recalled. He'd wrapped an arm around her shoulder until she'd stopped crying.

But he hadn't been with her on the last day of her life. In the weeks before her disappearance she'd telephoned him a few times—including the day before she died. He'd heard a break in her voice. Had she needed to cry that last day? Had she needed him?

Under his breath, he swore and jammed a foot on the accelerator, irritated he was dwelling on something he couldn't change. Why the overload of guilt this evening? Nothing could bring her back. Stupid. It was stupid to keep thinking about it. He eased his foot off the pedal. Speed wouldn't help, he reminded himself. He couldn't go fast enough to get away from his own thoughts.

Damn it, he should have been there for her, should have gone to her. *I'm sorry*. He wished he could say those words to her.

With the window cracked, he could smell the pines that bordered one side of the road. A chill still clung to the evening air in late May. Instinctively Max braked at a curve, but not soon enough. He caught a glimpse of an outline. Its doe eyes glazed, the deer had frozen, trapped in the beam of the headlights.

Gripping the steering wheel, Max veered right and faced inky darkness. As the car bounced over the shoulder of the road and the uneven ground that edged the dark woods, the silhouette of a tree trunk appeared. He saw it only a second before the car slammed into it. The air bag inflated, but his head whacked against the side window, snapped back, then hit again. So did his arm. Something cracked. A bone.

Max groaned, tried to reach up and touch his head. Pain shot through his arm. Nausea rose. With the side of his head pressed to the window, dizzy, he started to close his eyes. The last thing he saw was the silhouette of the deer dashing into the woods.

* * * *

Don't forget
RICH, RUGGED…RUTHLESS
is on the shelves now.

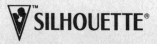